The Damsels from Derbyshire

The Damsels from Derbyshire

Ellen Fitzgerald

Walker and Company
New York

First published in the United States of America in 1992 by
Walker Publishing Company, Inc.
Published simultaneously in Canada by Thomas Allen & Son
Canada, Limited, Markham, Ontario

Library of Congress Cataloging-in-Publication Data
Fitzgerald, Ellen.
The damsels from Derbyshire : Ellen Fitzgerald.
ISBN 0-8027-1183-9
I. Title.
PR3569.T455D3   1992
813'.54—dc20   91-31856
CIP

Printed in the United States of America

2   4   6   8   10   9   7   5   3   1

Trip no further, pretty sweeting,
Journeys end in lovers meeting.

William Shakespeare,
Twelfth Night

The Damsels from Derbyshire

Prologue

THE KING'S THEATER WAS ablaze with lights from chandeliers and sconces. As usual, the house was filled to capacity, for the Italian Opera Company was in residence and the great Madame Catalani was singing the role of Euridice in Gluck's *Orfeo ed Euridice*. The first act had just drawn to a close, and the cheers and applause had finally died away.

Some of the audience were strolling about the house, commenting loudly on the performance, while others remained in their seats discussing the work or other members of the audience, such as the "Fashionable Impures." This group of ladies occupied a pair of boxes set side by side close to the stage, their jewels and low-cut gowns as well as the spurious bloom on their cheeks presenting a sad affront to the respectable ladies of the ton.

"If you will excuse me, my dearest Tabitha," a distinguished gentleman murmured to his daughter. "I have just seen a friend to whom I must speak."

"Of course, Papa." Eighteen-year-old Tabitha smiled at him, thinking how very handsome her papa was in his evening attire. She had seldom seen him looking so well and happy. She dutifully stifled the thought that she had seldom seen him at all in the past several years—not until this, her first Season in London. A vision of her mother rose in her mind's eye as she recalled one of their last conversations before her departure to London.

"No, my love, I will not be accompanying you," that lady had said firmly. "Such a pother, and the younger children need me much more than you do. Let dearest

Aunt Ellen be your chaperone. She truly enjoys such pleasures as the city offers. I do not."

Tabitha had been a little hurt by her mother's refusal, and she had wondered at it, as well. It had seemed to Tabitha that her mother must have wanted to visit London after spending most of her days in the wilds of Derbyshire. London was so thrilling. Her father would have welcomed her mother, she was sure, for when she had mentioned how seldom her father was home, he said apologetically, "It's dashed difficult to go back and forth to Derbyshire. The Prince Regent, you know."

The Earl of Sterling was a crony of the prince, and Tabitha supposed that His Royal Highness must want his friends with him. Yet, judging from the two or three times she had seen His Royal Highness, he had a great many friends about him and surely could have spared her father from time to time.

She decided to stop trying to fathom the royal desires and gazed at the adjoining boxes. Other gentlemen were leaving them, and below there was a similar exodus. Some of the men were entering other boxes where ladies held court.

Quite a few were hovering about the Fashionable Impures, and these ladies were evidently highly entertained by their sallies, for their laughter was loud, and one lady even went so far as to jab a gentleman with her fan. This scandalous behavior elicited Tabitha's aunt, the Honorable Ellen Parry, who had evidently been gazing in that same direction, even though she had adjured Tabitha not to look at them.

"Disgusting," she now commented, her small, pale blue eyes bright with disapproval, her thin, colorless lips turned down, and her long nose wrinkled as if she had just inhaled a particularly bad smell.

Tabitha's thoughts were abruptly terminated by a scratch on the door of their own box.

"Yes?" Miss Parry called.

The door was opened a crack. "May I please come in, Miss Parry?" a gentleman inquired rather shyly.

"Pray do," Tabitha said quickly and received a sharp, chiding glance from her aunt. However, Miss Parry merely said, "Please do, my lord."

The door was pulled fully open, and Lord Lovell appeared in the aperture. As he entered the box. Tabitha noticed that he was wearing the black and white evening attire favored by Beau Brummel. To her mind it was much more becoming than her father's peach-colored velvet suit and richly embroidered waistcoat.

The young man, heir to his father's title, Marquis of Ashton, was well above medium height, with dark eyes set in a classically handsome face. His hair, a rich brown, was brushed back from his forehead, save for a stray lock that had eluded the pomade and lay across his brow.

"Ma'am," he said respectfully, as he bowed over Miss Parry's hand. "I hope you are enjoying the opera?"

"Oh, yes, indeed. The works of Herr Gluck are much to my taste, Lord Lovell." Miss Parry smiled.

"And you, Lady Tabitha? I hope you are enjoying yourself. This is the first time you have heard Madame Catalani sing, or so your father tells me."

"Yes, it is," she said. "Her voice is so beautiful." Indicating her father's vacated chair, she added, "Will you not sit down, my lord?"

"I thank you." He took the proffered chair, his dark gaze never leaving her face. "It's uncommonly warm in the house tonight, do you not agree?"

"I do, indeed." Miss Parry moved forward. "It is a good thing the Season is drawing to a close."

"I am sure the performers would agree. It is probably twice as warm on stage."

"Oh, yes," Tabitha put in. "The performers must be very uncomfortable in those heavy costumes. The dancers must suffer even more, they are so active."

For some reason, Lord Lovell flushed. "Yes, I imagine so," he murmured.

"They do have compensations," Miss Parry commented dryly.

3

"Er . . . I rather think they do," he acknowledged, reddening slightly.

"Compensations?" Tabitha inquired. "I do not understand."

"They are generally paid quite handsomely," Lord Lovell explained hastily.

"Yes, quite," her aunt corroborated.

Tabitha was aware of something unspoken and wondered what it might be. There was a flush on her aunt's face, and though Lord Lovell was not flushing, his gaze, so frank and open on the other two occasions they had met, seemed now to be avoiding her own. A question trembled on her tongue, but she forgot it at the startling sound of a pistol shot directly below their box, coming, she thought, from the pit. Hastily, she leaned over the velvet-covered railing at the same time Lord Lovell and her aunt also stared into the pit.

With a quick thrust of his arm, Lord Lovell tried to push Tabitha back. Unfortunately, he was not in time to prevent her from seeing her father lying on his back in the aisle, a great stain of scarlet on his satin waistcoat.

From below, a cry still reverberated. "Take that, you damned seducer. May you rot in the hell where you belong!"

With shocked eyes, Tabitha saw a young man clutching a smoking pistol and standing over her father. "And now I'll be free of her," he declaimed in the tones of madness, and, placing the pistol against his head, he shot himself.

Too shocked to emulate her aunt's horrified scream, Tabitha felt as if she had been turned to stone. She was never sure how she was escorted hurriedly from the theater, for too many images crowded her mind, the first and foremost being that of her father lying so still on the floor, something her mind tried unsuccessfully to reject.

Her beloved father, whom she had seen so rarely in the past few years, had unaccountably been shot, had been murdered by an unknown assailant. Ringing in her ears was her aunt's scream followed by an incomprehensible, "It was bound to come to this. How could he be such a fool for a dancing girl?"

Just a short time ago, he had been sitting in his chair, applauding and smiling down at the stage. Had one of the girls in the ballet come very near to the side where their box was located, the first one in the row? Yes, Tabitha remembered. And then she forgot the thought as she realized a warm evening breeze was combing through her hair. How, she wondered, had she come to be outside? She had no recollection of leaving the theater.

"My carriage is near," Lord Lovell said. "Might I not take you home?" He looked at Tabitha and then at Miss Parry. His gaze strayed back to Tabitha.

"No, my lord, I do thank you." Miss Parry spoke with an unfamiliar crispness. "I am grateful for the offer, but I have sent for our own. It should be here directly. Come, my dear." Her hand closed hurtfully on Tabitha's arm, though her niece was sure that Miss Parry was unaware that she was inflicting pain, being as deep in shock as she was herself.

Lacing through that shock was a regret she feared to examine too closely—just as she feared to dwell on thoughts of her father. A fugitive memory presented him coming home after a day's shooting and snatching up a young Tabitha, giving her a great bear hug. "There's my beautiful girl," he had said warmly.

Tears blurred her vision and ran down her cheeks. Enmeshed in these memories, she was unaware of being helped into the carriage. It was only after the coachman began to maneuver the vehicle through the morass of other equipages also being hastily driven away from the theater, that she realized she had not said farewell to Lord Lovell.

Vainly, she threw a backward look out of the window, hoping to see him, but there were only other carriages, all seemingly leaving together. Then they were out of the morass and headed toward their house in Grosvenor Square.

* * *

The funeral service for Lord Sterling was held in the St. James's Church where he had attended Sunday services and where he had been married.

After the service, Tabitha escaped from those friends who gathered around herself and her aunt, hastily voicing expressions of sympathy.

"Air," she murmured, for the close summer heat of the church made her feel suffocated. Coming out onto the steps, she took long breaths. The air there was still hot, but fresher, she thought, than that inside.

"Lady Tabitha." A voice low and heavy with regret reached her. She looked back. On seeing Lord Lovell coming toward her, she felt an actual pain in her heart.

Meeting his anxious gaze, she said on a breath, "Lord Lovell."

"I have wanted to express my sympathies . . . but I was told you were not receiving callers," he said regretfully.

Who had told him that, she wondered indignantly, and knew of course that it had been her aunt. She longed to explain that those restrictions were none of her doing—but then Miss Parry was with her, giving Lord Lovell a censorious look and gripping Tabitha by the arm.

She uttered a curt acknowledgment of Lord Lovell's hastily spoken sympathies, directed to herself this time, and an answer to a question also directed to her aunt but meant, Tabitha was certain, for herself.

"No, my lord, we are not remaining in the city. We are bound for Derbyshire. We leave this afternoon."

"You will depart so soon?" he asked in some confusion.

"Indeed, yes," Miss Parry said brusquely. "My sister, Lady Sterling, will be much in need of comfort, and the children, too."

He flushed. "Of course, pray give them my deepest sympathies. My thoughts are with them, and you and . . . and Lady Tabitha, of course."

"Thank you, my lord," Miss Parry said crisply. Her clutch on Tabitha's arm tightened. "And now we must be going. Come, my dear."

Regret edged Tabitha's tone and found its way into her eyes. "Yes, Aunt Ellen," she said dutifully, wishing . . . but it was not a time for wishing. She had suffered a terrible loss. Why did she feel as if she was about to suffer another? If only they had known each other longer, she thought, but they had met only three times.

Softly, she said, "Farewell, my lord."

"Fare you well, Lady Tabitha," he said huskily. "May God be with you."

"And with you, my lord." She managed a tremulous smile and then surrendered to her aunt's now viselike grip on her arm. Dutifully, she walked away, but a lightning glance over her shoulder showed him still standing where she had left him, his eyes somber and his mouth grim.

═ 1 ═

"I HOPE AND PRAY that your sister Laura has learned her lesson," Miss Parry remarked acerbically. She paused and frowned. "However, I very much doubt it. A handful, that girl. What, I ask you, is to keep her from casting out lures to the next fortune hunter she meets? From what I understand—indeed, from what I have observed—London abounds with the breed!"

The two ladies sat in the parlor, waiting for the coach to be sent around. Laura had just run upstairs to make some just-thought-of adjustment to her costume.

Tabitha, knowing that her aunt was thinking of the trouble with a certain Frederick Perdue some three years ago when Laura was still a tender fifteen, said resignedly, "We will have to watch her carefully."

"Betsy has been warned," said Miss Parry in a low voice.

"She needs more than a mere abigail to watch her. A Bow Street Runner would have trouble keeping an eye on her," said Tabitha, trying to lighten her aunt's mood.

"Oh, dear," said Miss Parry. "Are we wise to take her to London?"

Tabitha wished she had not ventured her little joke. "Laura is rather fond of her creature comforts. I think she'll hold out for a rich husband, for all her talk of how she'll be the youngest of us to marry," she said comfortingly.

Then she thought of her oldest sister Alice, who had

married at twenty, and died ten years later, bearing a much-longed-for child. Not wanting to remind her aunt of the tragedy, she turned the subject slightly by adding, "With the two of us to watch her we should be able to prevent her from forming unsuitable attachments."

"There were plenty of people to watch her at that seminary in Bath, but she still managed to get into enough trouble that they requested you to take her away," Miss Parry commented acidly.

"I quite agree. Consequently, it remains for us to anticipate the worst and act accordingly." Tabitha sighed. "She's spent a quiet year at home. Surely that has sobered her."

Miss Parry shook her head. "I declare, I do not see how she comes by her devious ways. You were always such a biddable girl."

"I believe it was losing Papa in that horrid way and Mama falling into a decline." An image of her mother's stricken face as Miss Parry described the scene at the theater flickered before Tabitha's inner vision.

Though her aunt had not vouchsafed the true explanation for the slayer's actions, saying merely that Lord Gerald had been mad and dangerous, Lady Sterling had said bitterly, "I always knew he would come to grief over one or another of his females; he had no more discretion than an alley cat."

Tabitha remembered being shocked by that bitter and uncharacteristic comment. She was still shocked by it, wondering what dark wind had wafted the gossip to their corner of Derbyshire. And so quickly! However, it mattered little who had brought those ill tidings.

The damage was done, and her mother, always of uncertain health, had willed herself into the decline that killed her in a matter of two years. Tabitha had always suspected that her illness was based more on pride than grief, and Imogen, her sister, agreed.

"Mama could not bear the large doses of sympathy ladled out by various members of the family, not to mention our well-meaning neighbors," her youngest sister had said. "She had great pride, and to have Papa die in that horrid way and all the cartoonists making sport of the manner in which he was dispatched must have been very bitter for her."

Miss Parry's reply to Tabitha's previous statement interrupted her thoughts. "I blame William for leaving; he could have helped you and your poor mother bear the scandal," her aunt said.

"But he was newly married, and he has always preferred his holdings in Devon to the hills of Repton," Tabitha said, wishing that Aunt Ellen were a little less critical. She always worried so about the failings, real or imagined, of the family, while Tabitha always tried to present them in the best light.

But Tabitha had to admit she was rather annoyed with William. He had refused to let his wife even share the responsibility for Laura's debut, suggesting that Imogen would enjoy spending a Season in London. Suspecting that his rather spectacular losses at the gambling table prompted him to take this economy, Tabitha had not argued.

Nor had she asked Imogen, giving the excuse to William that their sister was occupied with her rapidly expanding nursery. Tabitha, with what help she could get from Aunt Ellen, must take on the task herself of seeing Laura settled.

She had thought of putting it off for a year in the hope that Laura would alter for the better, for despite her brave words to her aunt, she knew that Laura was likely to try to go her own way no matter what older and wiser heads advised.

However, she had decided that Laura's behavior would improve if she were to take on an adult role. Tabitha had tried to impress upon her sister that London Society was less tolerant of impropriety than the country, and Laura had promised to be good and a credit to the family.

Lost in thought, Tabitha was barely aware of a footman coming into the room and informing her aunt that the coach was waiting. Thinking of the conversation with Laura, she sighed. It would hardly be a difficult task to be a credit to the family, for they were a rather disreputable family. Only the scandal of her father's death could have overshadowed the scandal of her brother Henry's marriage. While still in mourning, Henry had eloped with the daughter of a wealthy cit.

At least James, happily reading classics at Cambridge, seemed to have no taste for scandal. But William's readiness to make a wager, and Henry's liking, despite his marriage, for flashy mistresses caused enough talk. And the death of their father was still talked about, so much, in fact, that Imogen refused to go to London except when necessary.

Nine years had passed since that terrible moment in the theater, and occasionally Tabitha wondered where the time had gone. In spite of all the responsibilities which had been her portion, she did not feel older in years. But she felt more deeply older in spirit.

Of course, she was no longer in her first youth, and, despite a number of offers, she had remained single, falling all too easily into the role of maiden aunt. This March, she had celebrated her twenty-seventh birthday, and she had already undertaken many responsibilities which previously would have been Aunt Ellen's lot. She had assisted at both Imogen's lyings-in, and she had recently learned there was to be another child in the late summer.

She hoped Laura would be creditably betrothed by then, or at least have formed a suitable attachment. It would make her life so much simpler. Seeing Laura married would be no easy task. Laura had been born as unpredictable as the March wind.

At least, and for this Tabitha was thankful, she would not have to undertake the task alone. Such a task should have been undertaken by a matron, either by William's wife or by Imogen, but, if assayed by an unmarried lady, must be done by one of maturer years than Tabitha. She had written to Aunt Ellen and, like a warhorse responding to the bugle's call, her aunt had arrived.

"Tabitha!"

A startled Tabitha looked at her aunt. "Yes, Aunt Ellen?"

"I vow you were woolgathering," accused Miss Parry.

"I am sorry. I was thinking."

"I hope you were devoting some of those thoughts to your sister. What a shame she is too old for leading strings. I do not look forward to this folly in London, I can tell you."

"No more do I," Tabitha admitted. She had long ago stopped expecting consistency from her aunt. Miss Parry would complain and sigh, but if it were suggested to her that the project be put off a year, she would not countenance it.

"I know the memories London holds for you and myself are hard to put aside." Her aunt shuddered. "But we must needs make the effort to see the chit settled. I pray no gossip attendant upon the Perdue episode reached London."

"I am sure it has not."

"Fifteen, if you please, and eloping with a fortune hunter. And he not yet of age!"

"Yes." Tabitha nodded and giggled.

"You find it amusing?" Miss Parry demanded, her eyes widening with outrage.

Meeting her aunt's disapproving stare, Tabitha hastily smoothed her smile away. Why did Frederick Perdue's youth so outrage her aunt? She said, "I am thinking of the look on his face when Henry and I met him at the door Laura had so thoughtfully left unbolted."

A small, unwilling smile curled the corners of Miss Parry's mouth. "It must have been a sad shock for him."

"It was. He kept looking at Henry and stuttering, 'But sir, but sir.' "

"I can't imagine why he refused that passage to India William offered him. It would have been an expense William should not have had to bear," Miss Parry said, "but one would hardly expect the child of an impoverished baronet to be sensible of that."

"I imagine he wanted to stay in England to find a wealthy bride. At least he seems to have kept his word and made no attempt to communicate with Laura. I expect she has forgotten about him by now."

"That girl, that girl. I do not look forward to London, I can assure you."

"Nor I," Tabitha agreed and bit down a sigh as an image of Lord Lovell flashed before her eyes, an image that had troubled her ever since she had refused an offer of marriage two months earlier. When she had first returned from London, pictures of Lord Lovell had haunted her waking and sleeping, but she had trained herself not to repine on him, for as the months went by it became clear that he was not waiting until the family was out of mourning; he was not waiting for anything. He had no intention, no reason for ever establishing contact with her.

And why should he? Theirs had been a brief friendship, felt very strongly on one side, and hardly at all on the other. She had not really thought of Lord Lovell for years. But when she had declined an offer of marriage for no better reason that that the man, a kind and considerate friend for many years, inspired only regard and esteem in her, she realized that she had put her heart into Lord Lovell's keeping and had been quite unable to take it back again.

"Tabitha!" Miss Parry snapped. I fear you will make a poor chaperone for your sister with this habit of falling into a virtual trance. As I have told you, I cannot bear the burden of Laura on my shoulders alone. I am not a young woman. I am close on fifty!"

Tabitha nodded, suddenly feeling sorry for her. Her aunt, the youngest child in her family by a number of years, had grown up the only plain daughter in a family of beauties. It had been assumed she would never marry. From the age of ten she had happily made her home with her eldest married sister, a welcome companion in a childless home. And then, after several years of marriage, and at the advanced age of thirty-six, her sister, like poor Alice, had died bearing her first child.

Ellen had stayed with her brother-in-law, looking after her little niece until he remarried. Then she had returned to her parents. After being for some years a companion to her elderly and increasingly difficult mother, she had subsequently become the family chaperone and aunt-of-all-work, going from sister to brother, wherever she was needed. She did not even have her own house, although her eldest brother, with self-conscious and conspicuous generosity, made a virtue of the courtesy of letting her keep the rooms she had occupied while her father was still alive.

No wonder, thought Tabitha, that she prefers to keep traveling. I must ask William if she can spend the winter here. Perhaps she would even like to live here.

Before her aunt could assume her mind was wandering again, Tabitha said, "I will be sure to keep an eye on Laura, Aunt Ellen. I am quite aware that she has a strong partiality for mischief."

"Indeed, she does." Miss Parry shook her head. "I need not say which member of the family she favors."

"No," Tabitha admitted ruefully. "She and Henry could be twins."

"I was not thinking of Henry," Lady Ellen said sharply. "I was thinking of your father, whom both Henry and Laura resemble in character, if not appearance. I have never ceased to be grateful that your poor mother died before Henry eloped with that misbegotten female . . . what's her name? The potter's daughter?"

"Joan's father *owns* a pottery, Aunt Ellen. He is exceedingly wealthy. And his Joan was born several years after her parents married."

"He started his life as a potter," Miss Parry insisted, ignoring the reference to the circumstance of Joan's conception.

"No, on the contrary, he was educated at Shrewsbury." Tabitha liked her brother's father-in-law, rather better than some of her own relations if the truth be told. "He went into the pottery to learn the trade so he could continue the business begun by his father, who *was* a potter."

"I do not care to be corrected in that way, Tabitha."

"I am sorry if I distressed you, Aunt. It is just that from what Henry told me and I have observed, his father-in-law is very gentlemanly and extremely astute."

"If he is so 'extremely astute,' how can he stomach Henry?" Miss Parry demanded. Without waiting for an answer, she continued. "But I imagine the fact that Henry is 'the Honorable' and the younger son of an earl covers a multitude of his many sins. A man like him would enjoy hearing his daughter called the Honorable Mrs. Spencer."

"I expect it must," Tabitha agreed ruefully.

"Still," Miss Parry added, shaking her head, "that poor girl . . . three children in as many years and Henry . . ."

"And Laura could be his twin. Both charming and both self-absorbed."

"I do not like to think of Laura in London." Miss Parry began the familiar litany again.

"We must hope for the best," Tabitha said firmly. "I do wish Mama had lived, though. She could always handle Laura. Even as a child, she was difficult. I suppose we spoiled her since she was the last baby."

The hall clock chimed nine times. "Oh, dear, it is nearly time to leave," she sighed.

"And may God have mercy on us," Miss Parry said prayerfully.

"Indeed," her niece agreed. "At least," she added, "I will finally be seeing London again, and this time I mean to take advantage of what the city offers."

"And what may that be, pray?"

"Museums and art galleries. I mean to visit as many as possible." And, she thought to herself, exorcise the ghost of Lord Lovell. I can't spend another year moping after him as I did when I was eighteen.

"Not with Laura in tow," Miss Parry exclaimed. "She'll never stand for it."

"I trust," Tabitha said dryly, "that I will have some time to myself. If you could manage for a morning or two on your own. . . ."

"We will see." An ominous note had entered Miss

Parry's voice. "Your sister is a handful, or rather she is too much for one pair of hands or eyes. You must keep that in mind, my love."

Tabitha nodded. "I assure you that the probability of difficulties with Laura is well implanted in my thinking. But I wonder if we are making too much of it. Yes, Laura is self-centered, and yes, she has been foolish, but perhaps we are borrowing trouble. I expect that the excitement of London will take the edge off her mischief. She does like fun, and if occupied she won't have to make her own."

"She has a great capacity for enjoyment. So did you once, my love." Miss Parry gave her a probing look. "I would have thought you'd have been married by now, not buried in the dull countryside. You did not want for offers."

"You know I could not leave the family," Tabitha said defensively.

"Could not . . . would not." Miss Parry surveyed her from narrowed eyes. "Indeed."

"The coach is at the door!" Laura, as fair and as beautiful but more vivacious than her sister Tabitha, danced into the chamber. "The horses are fretting, straining at their bits. Do let's go! I have been waiting for this moment all my life."

Miss Parry exchanged a glance with Tabitha, and both ladies burst into laughter, much to Laura's confusion.

"I cannot see what amuses you," she said a shade crossly. She darted a glance at her sister out of eyes the same color and fringed by the same dark lashes as those of Tabitha. The gaze, however, was patently different— one alight with eagerness and the other coolly resigned.

=== 2 ===

"To LONDON," CRIED LAURA excitedly. "And no more than two days' distance!"

"Depending upon the weather," reminded Miss Parry.

"Oh, it is summer and it is bound to be fine," Laura said positively. "Come, do come, I can't bear to wait any longer."

Her eagerness was infectious. Tabitha, who had been looking rather somber, smiled. "Neither can I." She could tell from her aunt's pursed lips that Miss Parry was about to comment that it was Laura who had kept them waiting, not the other way around, and, to forestall this, she opened the door, saying, "After you, Aunt Ellen."

Miss Parry, followed by her nieces, left the breakfast parlor. The ladies moved toward the front door where their abigails were waiting to assist them into the huge traveling coach awaiting them.

Laura, however, did not immediately join her sister and her aunt. Instead she moved nearer the box of the equipage and sent a pleading look up at Bartlett, the coachman. "You will hurry, will you not?" she wheedled. "It should not take us more than two days to reach London, should it?"

He gave her an indulgent smile. " 'Tis the weather to which ye must apply, yer ladyship. Me'n the 'orses'll do us best for ye."

"I give you leave to drive through the rain if any falls," Laura cried. "But it won't, I shan't allow it."

"Come, Laura. Bartlett won't thank you for that permission," called Tabitha. "Come, take your place."

"Such nonsense you do speak," Miss Parry reproved Laura, as, aided by a smiling footman, the girl climbed into the coach.

"It-mustn't-rain, it-mustn't-rain," Laura repeated as if it were a charm. She took a seat by the window saved for her by Tabitha, who had resigned herself to sitting between her sister and her aunt. She hoped devoutly that the roads would not be too rough, and hoped also that given the fine weather that was part of the early summer's bounty, the journey would be less wearisome than she anticipated.

For several hours the ladies amused themselves in conversation, then began playing a Spencer family game, that of having to string together quotations by association. Tabitha enjoyed herself until Laura recited, "Journey's end in lovers' meetings."

"Journeys end in lovers' meetings." Tabitha winced. The quotation carried with it the all-too-vivid image of Lord Lovell. Firmly, she told herself that he must have changed in nine years. She must stop this foolish infatuation. She was twenty-seven, not eighteen, and her life had been very full without the impossible love of Lord Lovell. He had not, she reminded herself, made any effort to see her. If he had wanted to, surely he could have found friends in Derbyshire to visit.

But he hadn't. He had simply lived his own life, without any interest in sharing it with her. And she must concentrate on the fact that he had *never* wanted to share it with her. He would have found a lady he cared for, and by now must be the father of a young family. He would have had to marry, for he had been the only son of an only son, and the succession, if not his natural inclinations, would have demanded it. And she knew that he was fond of children.

She recalled him mentioning his little sister, his only sibling. Undoubtedly this sister, Katherine, was now a young lady. Hastily, Tabitha arrested her musings. She was letting her thoughts wander away from her subject, which was to recall her few conversations with Lord Lovell.

Tabitha was about to enter the game again, since both Miss Parry and Laura had paused when there was a distant rumble of thunder.

"Oh, dear," said Laura in the accents of tragedy, "it cannot, cannot rain!"

However, it did rain; the silvery sheets pelted against the coach windows. Soon there was thunder and lightning, unsettling the horses.

Rapping on the roof of the coach to attract Bartlett's attention, Miss Parry demanded to know whether there was a decent inn anywhere near.

" 'Bout a good mile down the road, ma'am, there's a decent little house called the Golden Bell."

For two days they remained in the cramped accommodations of the little inn. Caught between her aunt's increasingly irritable disposition and Laura's sulks, Tabitha was thankful when between one hour and the next, the rain finally ceased.

Under way once again, they made good time till they reached the outskirts of London. There they were slowed down on streets crowded by drays, wagons, gigs, curricles, and oversized coaches near in shape and size to their own.

The shrill cries of street vendors were heard above the rumbling of the traffic, inviting the public to purchase meat pies, to have scissors ground, to purchase broadsides, to eat fresh baked buns, to buy all manner of fruits—sounds that all blended into a meaningless roar.

Miss Parry defensively clapped her hands to her heart, but Laura listened excitedly, adding her own voice to the welter of sounds as she pointed out one or another strange-looking peddler, or a fashionable gown, or a tall house or church. Her face was pressed against the window, and she was suddenly loudly and lewdly hailed by a well-dressed man. Angrily, Miss Parry pulled her back.

"Sit down and behave."

Sulkily, Laura did as she was told. "I was only trying to see."

"And you were seen!"

Trying to prevent another ugly spat, Tabitha reverted to the quotations game. *"Veni, vidi, vici."*

"And just see if I don't," Laura said with a touch of defiance.

I have no doubt you will conquer all you meet, thought Tabitha, regarding her sister fondly. Despite the rigors of the journey, Laura looked fresh and young and excited.

Tabitha had a moment of wishing that time could be rolled back to her own sadly aborted Season. Had she remained longer . . . With an angry shake of her head she thrust the foolish thought from her mind.

Just then the coach turned into Grosvenor Square and drew to a stop in front of a red brick mansion, which rose three stories to a flat roof. The front door, painted green, was flanked by a pair of oblong windows. The house, she remembered, had always been pleasantly light inside.

"I do not remember the door being green," Miss Parry commented.

"I expect it has been newly painted," Laura said. "I like it."

Tabitha laughed. Whatever impetuous qualities marred Laura's character, she was blessed with enthusiasm and a delight in life. "You are primed to like everything about the house and the town."

"I, myself," put in Miss Parry, "like the idea of resting after the exigencies of the journey, and I must advise both of you to follow my example. Our days until Laura's presentation will be full, and afterward I certainly do not anticipate the pace will slacken."

Tabitha was overcome with a sense of déjà vu. She was certain she had heard those words before. Then it came to her. She remembered her own arrival at the house, nine years earlier with her aunt. Miss Parry had given her the same advice as they arrived. Advice which, she thought wryly, she had welcomed no more than Laura.

Immediately Laura said, echoing Tabitha's own words of that earlier occasion and thus adding to the feeling, "I do not want to rest. I am not in the least bit weary."

The door of the coach opened, and the steps set against its side. Laura, the first out, hurried down them and ran up the stairs to the front door. She was followed less swiftly by Miss Parry and Tabitha.

"I declare, I am already weary just at the *thought* of keeping up with Laura," Miss Parry commented.

"Perhaps she will calm down after a week or so. We must remember that this is all new to her," Tabitha said.

"Or in a month or six." Miss Parry cast her eyes heavenward. "Laura has always darted about like a mayfly, though given some of her scrapes she might be more accurately compared to a dragonfly."

"It is natural she should be excited," Tabitha said. "London is all so new and different for her, as it would be for anyone who has spent their entire life in the country."

Before Miss Parry could reply, Laura seized the knocker on the front door and slammed it hard against its plate.

"I am sure that sound must have been heard through the whole house," Miss Parry said disapprovingly. "Laura, as always, you are far too precipitate."

"I do not see why we should be standing out here, when we could be inside," Laura replied with a mischievous giggle.

Miss Parry was prevented from commenting by the opening of the door.

"Ah," she said to the tall dark man in footmen's livery who stood in the doorway. "Good afternoon. I am Miss Parry."

"Good afternoon, ma'am," he said, flushing slightly. "You are in good time."

"I, for one, do not think we are in good time," Laura said. "We were held up on the road for days and days by the wretched rain."

He nodded again. "I am sorry to hear that, miss."

"I am Lady Laura," she put in sharply.

"I beg your pardon, your ladyship."

"Are you going to keep us here all day?" Laura demanded, pushing past him.

He moved aside so that Miss Parry and Tabitha could follow. "I beg your pardon, but could I ask you to wait in the drawing room?"

"Is anything the matter?" Tabitha asked, wondering at his hesitation.

"My question also." Miss Parry nodded. "What is amiss, young man?"

"Mr. Henry is staying here, ma'am."

"Henry," Laura cried, in accents of delight. "Oh is he? But of course, where else would he be at this time of year?" She ran up the stairs, calling for her brother.

"Where is he?" demanded Miss Parry.

"In the library, ma'am. I think you should stop the young lady, ma'am. Mr. Henry . . . well, ma'am, you see, Mr. Henry, he isn't exactly alone."

Tabitha, not certain what was troubling the servant, hurried up the stairs, calling for Laura to return. She could hear her aunt questioning the footman. "Females?"

"Yes, ma'am." And then, as if in mitigation, "But Lord Ashton is with them, ma'am."

"Laura, Tabitha, come back at once," demanded Miss Parry.

But it was too late. A door opened, a slender young man in his early twenties stepped out, and Laura ran to embrace him.

Tabitha had stopped at her aunt's order, but now went forward again. She put out a hand to stop her sister, but Laura went in the room, pulling Henry by the hand. Sighing, Tabitha followed her.

There were five people in the room. Henry and Laura stood just inside the door. Near the fireplace were two slender young women clad in silk gowns. And by a table, on which lay a spill of cards, stood another man, who was turning to face the door as Tabitha entered. On seeing her, he stopped moving, his eyes widening.

He looked older—that was the first thing which occurred to her. The second was that she must look older to him. The third was that if she was seven and twenty, he must be three and thirty. The fourth was that she should not stand there doing mental arithmetic.

"Lord Lovell," she said in a low voice.

"Lady Tabitha." He moved quickly to her side and took the hand she offered him, bringing it to his lips.

"Lord Lovell," cried Miss Parry as she bustled into the room.

"He's Ashton now," Henry interpolated. "Afternoon, Auntie."

"How pleasant to see you again, ma'am." Lord Ashton held Tabitha's hand a second longer before relinquishing it to greet her aunt.

"Lord, Aunt Ellen," Henry commented wryly, "you must have made poor old Bartlett drive as if the devil himself were after you. I never knew you were one for speed."

"We went ever so slowly," Laura said, "and there was that horrid rainstorm." She pouted prettily, then smiled at Lord Ashton.

"Still," said Miss Parry, "it only made the journey more wearisome. The roads were rough."

"I enjoyed every minute of it—" Laura said with a wild disregard for both the truth and the fact that her aunt had not finished speaking, "—because we were coming to London. London! And now I am here." Again she bestowed a smile upon Lord Ashton.

"I am glad you are ready to enjoy London. It can be a wonderful city. Mr. Boswell once wrote to the effect that when a man is tired of London, he is tired of life."

"Oh, I have wanted all my life to visit. But, my lord, I had no idea you were so apt with quotations. You must come to visit and play the game with us."

"Laura," said Miss Parry sharply, "I think it is a little premature of you to be issuing invitations. And I am certain that Lord Ashton has not the least idea of or interest in what you are prattling about. As I was saying, it was a very rough journey, and we must retire to rest."

"I just want a cup of tea," Laura said, sitting down.

With a tact Tabitha did not expect in one of her profession, one of the girls by the fireplace said, "You must excuse me, if you please, but it becomes late, and we must rehearse."

"Yes," said the other girl, in accented English. "Our rehearsal, it starts soon."

They were about to slip past the ladies when Laura cried, "Henry, where are your manners? Do introduce me to your friends."

Miss Parry turned pale.

Henry gulped like a fish.

"Forgive me," said Lord Ashton. "Miss Parry, allow me to present Mademoiselle Duboise and Mademoiselle Durand, of the Royal Opera Ballet."

Henry, who seemed to think that in for a penny in for a pound, said, "And these are m'sisters, Lady Tabitha and Lady Laura." Catching sight of his aunt's face, he added, "And you must excuse me while I summon Ashton's rig."

"And I shall escort the mademoiselles downstairs," Ashton said.

Ashton, Henry, and the two women left the room. Miss Parry looked at Tabitha with exasperation writ large upon her features. She was about to comment, but was forestalled by Laura, who, turning to Tabitha, said excitedly, "I collect you are acquainted with Lord Ashton. What a handsome man! And I think he likes me. He was most complimentary, don't you think?"

"I think," said Miss Parry, "that he made a few commonplace remarks suitable to a young girl just out of the schoolroom."

"Oh, I think it was a great deal more than that. I could tell that he seemed quite, quite taken with me." Laura spun around and made an expansive curtsy.

"And you are quite, quite too full of yourself," her aunt snapped. "It cannot have escaped your attention that I was trying to leave the room without forcing upon the gentlemen the embarrassment of introducing those creatures."

"Oh, those pretty women from the opera ballet? I have been given to understand that all gentlemen keep them." Laura giggled. "I suppose they think it adds to their consequence to be seen with a lovely woman."

"And where did you receive this fine understanding?" Miss Parry demanded.

"Henry told me ages ago."

"I am extremely surprised at him," Miss Parry snapped. "That is knowledge of a sort most improper for young girls."

"But I wanted to know about Papa," Laura began.

"That is quite enough." Miss Parry gave her pert niece a quelling glare. "In future you will pay attention to the conversation of your elders so that you may follow their lead. And now, go to your room and rest."

"I am not tired," Laura said. "But," she added, seeing that her aunt was in no mood for further impertinences, "I do wish to see to the unpacking of my garments. I wonder where Betsy has gone. I wish we might hire an abigail here. She would be sure to be more knowledgeable than Betsy."

"You would do well not to look any further than Betsy," Miss Parry said dampeningly. "Her knowledge is quite sufficient for your needs, and she is skilled at hairdressing as few are."

"That is true, my dear," Tabitha assured her, knowing full well that while Betsy could dress hair beautifully, her chief recommendations where Laura were concerned were her sharp mind and the fact that she was young enough to keep up with her mistress and old enough not be awed into obeying foolish orders.

"If I had your girl, I'd not complain," Laura said. "Might we not exchange maids? I mean, just while we are in London."

"No, that is out of the question," Tabitha said firmly. "Jane has been with me for close on to ten years. I doubt she would appreciate the change in positions."

Laura shrugged. "What can it matter what *she* appreciates or does not appreciate? She will lose nothing in the way of remuneration and she will be in the same household, but I can see you are quite determined on retaining her. Do tell me about Henry's friend. Did you see him often when you were first in London? He is certainly a handsome man."

"For my part," Miss Parry said tartly, "I scarcely recognize him. And I thought, Laura, that you were going to your chamber."

"Well then, I'm gone," said Laura, and flounced out of the room.

Miss Parry sat down and untied the strings to her plain brown bonnet. "I simply cannot cope with that child. And what is Henry doing here? Does he never remain at home?"

"Judging from his wife's letters, I would think not," Tabitha commented dryly. She went over to the table on which lay the cards. They were dealt out for a three-handed game. Idly she tidied them into a neat pile.

"Such an unmitigated scapegrace, carrying on in this house in such a fashion."

"Are you talking of me, Auntie, or Ashton?" said Henry as he reentered the library.

"I could be speaking of anyone, Henry, who is caught up in the fast life of London."

Henry frowned. "If Ashton has been caught up in the fast life of London, as you please to term it, he can hardly be blamed for it."

"Of course *you* would defend him," replied Miss Parry sarcastically.

"Anyone who knew him well would defend him if they knew the whole story."

"The . . . whole story?" Tabitha questioned. "What might that be?"

"Five years ago he married a very beautiful young widow, a few years his senior. William knew her, told me she was exquisite. Unfortunately, she died at the birth of her first child, and the infant was stillborn."

"Oh," said Tabitha in some distress. "I did not know."

"How could you know, my dear?" said Miss Parry. "You didn't keep up with any of your London acquain-

26

tances, and you hardly knew Lord Lovell—Lord Ashton, that is. And you never read the papers."

"Point is, Auntie, the girls are m'friends. Ashton doesn't go in for that sort of thing anymore. He came to see when you would be arriving."

"Why?" asked Tabitha.

"How should I know? Heard through some friend of William's that you were coming to town."

Miss Parry fixed Henry with a gimlet eye. "I think, Henry, that you had better find other accommodation."

Henry regarded her with an amazement strongly colored with annoyance. "Why should I find other accommodation, Auntie? This is William's house and I have his permission to use it whenever I want. You and m'sisters also use it with his permission. I have as much right as you to stay in this house."

"But not to bring opera dancers here. Do you consider them fit company for ladies of quality, and your sisters at that?" Miss Parry demanded.

"Had I known you would be arriving today, they'd not have been here," he retorted with righteous indignation.

"You knew we were coming. You knew when," she snapped.

"I allowed for the exigencies of travel on the roads, especially in the rain. No matter, they will not be invited here again. And though you might not be aware of it, I can be of use to you."

"Indeed? I cannot imagine how." Miss Parry regarded him with a skeptical eye.

Tabitha jumped into the conversation before her aunt could continue. "Yes, indeed, Henry! I would deeply appreciate some masculine support. I begged William to come, even if only for a fortnight since Matilda did not care to, but he felt he could not leave Devon just now."

"Ah." Henry smiled at Tabitha. "You do need me. And until you are better acquainted with the town, you'll need me in other ways that you had not thought. Have any of you a notion where the best mantua-makers are to be found? Or milliners? I know them all."

"I am sure you do," Miss Parry said coldly, not liking to be bested. "We will not inquire how you came by this fine knowledge."

"Also bootmakers," Henry continued, unabashed. "And there are bazaars where you can buy gloves, parasols, and ribbons, not to ignore the Circassian corset, invented by the good Mrs. Bell."

"Henry!" Miss Parry glared at him. "The idea of mentioning the—"

"Unmentionables?" He grinned. "But are they not needed, too?"

"Henry!" In spite of her best efforts, Tabitha was laughing. "Enough! We believe you are sufficiently knowledgeable for our purposes, and certainly you may stay." She turned to her aunt. "We are two against your one, Aunt Ellen, and you must admit that Henry knows his way around the city. His lending us escort will be very comfortable."

Miss Parry frowned and looked as if she were about to offer another argument. Then she sighed and said, "So be it. I am outnumbered. You may stay, but please, Henry, no more opera dancers here."

"You have my sacred word."

Just then a footman entered with a tray of tea and biscuits, which had been ordered, he told them, by Lady Laura for Miss Parry and Lady Tabitha. Henry took his leave, and Tabitha poured cups of tea for her aunt and herself.

"Laura is trying to be thoughtful, Aunt Ellen."

"I wish she would be thoughtful at the time, and not need to try to make amends later. I vow, half her troubles are her impetuousness. If only she could learn to think first. If she thought less of herself and more of others . . ." Miss Parry continued her analysis of Laura's character.

Tabitha was thinking of Lord Ashton. He was older, sadder somehow. Even before Henry had told her the pitiful history of Lord Ashton's marriage, she had been aware of an air of melancholy in his expression that had been lacking nine years ago. No, she had seen it once, on the day they parted at the church. She remembered those moments all too clearly, remembered too, that they had passed far too quickly.

She had thought about Lord Ashton all the way to London, despite her best efforts not to, and she had wondered if they would meet. Well, they had met, and she had seen nothing in his manner to suggest that she was anything to him but a distant acquaintance . . . yet he had called to see when they would arrive. And she would not make too much of that. She was too old to let her heart be broken again.

= 3 =

IN THE SENNIGHT FOLLOWING their arrival in London, Tabitha woke each morning to days filled with appointments at mantua-makers, bootmakers, and milliners.

On their first free morning, Henry went to collect the jewelry that had been sent out to be cleaned. The ladies waited for him in the back parlor, a pleasant, sunny room, talking about the gowns they had commissioned.

"And when we see these garments finished, the eleventh of May and the Presentation will be upon us," said a weary Miss Parry to an equally weary Tabitha. Presiding over Laura's fittings, Tabitha had had many an argument persuading her sister that the purples and red that her taste ran to were not *comme il faut* for a girl in her first season.

"They will make you exceptional," she had unwisely said.

"But I want to be exceptional," Laura had replied.

Finally, Tabitha had pointed out that such strong colors sadly diminished the effect of Laura's delicate porcelain complexion and silver-gilt hair.

The mantua-maker, one Mrs. Noble, had agreed with Tabitha, and even Henry—who, at Laura's request, had come to view the materials in question—had also pronounced himself entirely in agreement with Laura's antagonists. His championship caused a grateful Miss Parry to refrain from mentioning the fact that Henry appeared on suspiciously good terms with the mantua-maker.

Mrs. Noble's warm welcome had, in fact, been duplicated in several other establishments. Remembering this, Miss Parry commented, "My heart goes out to Henry's poor young wife."

"That was not what you said when Henry eloped with the chit." Laura laughed. "To my thinking it was a fair exchange. She has the pleasure of being the Honorable Mrs. Henry Spencer, which may mean slightly more to her than to have Henry rusticating in the country."

"We should not be his judges," Tabitha responded. "Particularly when he has been so very helpful. He has, you know . . . must agree with me. Indeed, I do not know what we could have done without him."

"No more do I," Henry commented, walking in on this conversation. He was carrying several small leather cases which he set down on a nearby table.

"Oh, would those be the jewels?" Laura cried. "What have you for me?"

"This, m'dear." He handed her a box. "Do be careful how you open it, child." He turned to Tabitha. "And this, m'love, is for you."

Opening her box, Laura said disappointedly, "Pearls, and so very small."

"They are matched and quite perfect, born of an oyster's agony. I suppose you would prefer rubies? I must tell you, infant," Henry grinned at her, "that they are not at all the thing for little girls."

"I am eighteen!" she snapped.

"Precisely."

"Oh!" Laura said crossly, and then in a very different tone, "Oh," as she gazed at the necklace Tabitha had taken from her box.

It consisted of exquisitely carved cameos framed in gold and hung on a delicate gold chain with a tiny pearl between each. "I would much prefer those to pearls. Might we not exchange necklaces, Tabitha?"

Tabitha remembered when she had first worn the cameo necklace—at Almack's. Lord Lovell—Lord Ashton, she reminded herself—had requested a dance—a cotillion, and she had shyly put his name down in her program. She had thought that he was the most handsome young man she had ever seen. Even today, he was still very handsome. The years had changed him, true, but they had not robbed him of his striking good looks.

"May I have the necklace?" Laura asked eagerly, lifting it from the box where her sister had just laid it. "Oh, I do love it!"

"No," Tabitha responded, suddenly angry at Laura's all-pervasive selfishness. "Grandfather gave it to me, and in his memory I will wear it."

"He was my grandfather, too," Laura pouted. "Please, Tabitha, it would be so very becoming to me."

"No," Tabitha said coolly, her resolve hardening. "In fact, I think I will have a gown made, in amber silk. They should look very well together."

"I do think you are being amazingly selfish," Laura said pettishly. "Anyone would think it was you who were being presented. That event happened ten years ago. You're too old for pretty gowns."

"That does not make Tabitha in her dotage," Henry said. He rolled his eyes. "Lord, such controversy over a necklace! Pearls are infinitely more proper for you, infant, and very becoming with your pretty complexion."

"I am not an infant!" Laura snapped. "I am turned eighteen, you'll recall."

"Then stop behaving like an eight-year-old." Her brother laughed.

"Quite!" Miss Parry agreed. "Laura, one more word from you and you can spend the rest of the morning in your room. Let us examine the rest of the jewels."

However, later in the privacy of Tabitha's chamber, she said, "I cannot quite understand why you would not give in to the child on the matter of the necklace. There is no use being selfish and, after all, youth must be served."

"What you really mean is that Laura must be served because you can't bear the thought of one of her tantrums," Tabitha said coldly. "That's not the way to teach her to behave. Well, you may placate her if you must, but not with my necklace."

"I do not understand you. Truly, I don't. This is a great event in Laura's life, and the necklace, while beautiful, is such a trifle."

"Not to me. I feel strongly about it and do not wish to hear another word on the subject, Aunt Ellen," Tabitha said.

"As you wish, but still I do not understand you. It is not like you to make such a pother over nothing."

"So you have already said," Tabitha replied wearily. "Pray let there be an end to this discussion."

"You are pleased to be so stubborn." Miss Parry frowned. "I do not know you in this mood!" Turning on her heel, she left the chamber, much to her niece's relief.

It was only then that she opened the box again and looked at the necklace, planning the new gown in her mind. But instead unbidden images flowed into her thoughts.

He had been shy and hesitant. When he had asked if he might be her partner in the cotillion, she, dazzled by his handsome face, had been equally shy in her acquiescence. They had not spoken much, but when he had escorted her back to Aunt Ellen and had bowed his farewell, she suddenly had felt bereft.

What was the use in remembering? It was more than merely water under the bridge. Her meeting with him, two weeks ago, had proved that a veritable ocean flowed between them. Her feelings appeared to remain unchanged, and so did those of Lord Lovell. He, and her foolish *tendre,* were a part of her own vanished youth, never to be seen again.

She wished strongly that she had never come to London. However—her weary mind circled back again— Laura had to have her come-out and Aunt Ellen couldn't possibly handle her alone. So there was no sense in bewailing her fate.

"Oh, oh, oh! I am so glad that the ordeal is over!" Laura cried as, unmindful of her white silk gown with its cumbersome hoops and long train, she scrambled from the coach, ignoring the footman waiting to hand her down.

"I beg you will not let your train drag on the ground," Miss Parry called in long-suffering tones.

"Do try for a little conduct," Tabitha added sharply.

"Oh, very well." Laura looped the train over her arm, then ran up the steps to the front door, where the footman was waiting to admit them.

"Such energy," Miss Parry remarked in an exhausted tone of voice. "The child comported herself very well, I thought."

"Very well," Tabitha agreed. "Her curtsy was uncommonly graceful."

"The Prince Regent had an eye for her, unless I am deeply mistaken."

"Possibly," Tabitha said, remembering that nine years ago, *she* had been presented to the king and queen. His Majesty had startled her with a "What, what, what!" addressed loudly to a flustered Queen Charlotte. It was fortunate for Laura that tonight she had not had the poor old king staring at her and clutching her hand in his hard grip, for she would very likely have answered him.

"The Regent is very gracious," she said.

"He has gained weight. They say he wears a corset," Miss Parry remarked.

"Yes," Tabitha agreed rather ruefully, remembering that nine years ago he had been much less plump and, accordingly, much more handsome.

"I am glad not only that Laura behaved so creditably, but also that it is over."

"Indeed," Tabitha agreed. "The place was sadly overheated."

"Was it not! The windows tight shut. They say the Regent has a great fear for his health. Ah, well, that is over and I would the Season were, too."

"Yes." Tabitha sighed. "I quite agree."

"You really should not agree, my dear." Miss Parry shook her head. "You are looking very well, you know. I am sure the Regent thought so, too."

"The . . . Regent?" Tabitha repeated incredulously.

Her aunt nodded. "He looked at you more than once. Did you not notice?"

"No, I was watching Laura," Tabitha said.

"Well, you may take it from me, my dear, he looked at you and with *considerable* interest. Which, of course, does not surprise me. You wear your years most becomingly."

Tabitha bit down a burgeoning laugh. It was as close to a compliment as she was ever likely to receive from her aunt, and she was rather sure that without the supposed sanction of the Regent, it was one Miss Parry would not have uttered.

Though Tabitha had very little in the way of conceit and had believed herself long separated from the beauty she was said to have possessed as a young girl, it was pleasant to hear that some small part of it remained.

Still, despite her aunt's encomium, she felt all of her twenty-seven years this day. Aside from the heat of the palace and the amount of time that passed before Laura was presented, she had found herself most inopportunely dwelling on Lord Lovell, Lord Ashton rather, older and wiser in the ways of the world and, like herself, no stranger to tragedy.

Indeed, she had been so concentrated on her thoughts that she had hardly heard her sister's name announced. She wondered now if their paths would cross again. But, she reminded herself, such speculations were hardly necessary. The polite world was small, and Lord Ashton was, after all, a friend of her brother. She should not indulge in such speculations. It was inevitable that they would see each other, but they would not see each other as they had nearly a decade ago; that went without saying.

I do not love Lord Ashton, I do not love Lord Ashton, she repeated to herself as they entered the house. .

As Tabitha had promised herself, she had ordered a gown made to complement her necklace. Fashioned of amber and ivory silk, it was, she thought, very elegant and set off the necklace quite as effectively as she had hoped.

Tonight would see Laura's debut at Almack's. Tabitha had been fortunate that her father had been a great favorite with the Countess de Lieven. Using this as a lever, Tabitha had been able to persuade the powerful patronesses to provide them with vouchers, even though Mrs. Drummond-Burrell was known already to have stigmatized Laura as hoydenish.

Jane had dressed her hair à la Greque. Tabitha wondered whether some Grecian goddess, magically wafted down from Mount Olympus, would have recognized Jane's adaption. She smiled derisively. Her thoughts were traveling in many directions this evening, skirting the one topic she must needs ignore.

"Oh, milady," Jane breathed. "You are a picture."

"If indeed I am, you have painted it," Tabitha said, kindly.

" 'Tis not hard to dress your hair, milady. It is so beautiful and yet not so fine that it eludes the combs."

"I have always been glad of that," Tabitha said.

"You should be, milady," Jane assured her. "And if you'll allow me the liberty, you do look shining tonight."

"Shining?" Tabitha repeated. "What can you mean, Jane?"

" 'Tis like how you looked when you was first in London—you shone, milady." Jane flushed. "If you'll not mind me telling you so."

"Mind? How would I mind?" Tabitha smiled. "It is a great compliment, and I do thank you for it."

She was suddenly reminded of the first time she had been dressed to go to Almack's. Jane had been similarly complimentary that time, too. Then, unbidden, an image of her father, who had escorted her there, rose in her mind's eye.

He had been in no very good humor, complaining about the knee-breeches which were de rigueur for those gentlemen who attended the subscription dances.

"Petty tyranny," he had rasped. "Those toplofty hostesses comport themselves like the queen, herself, save that she is considerably less full of herself. Knee-breeches, indeed! We are not living in the time of George II."

She had said, "But, Papa, you have such shapely legs. Why do you disdain knee-breeches?"

He had laughed and called her a sly puss. She shook her head, not wanting to indulge in the inevitable train of memories that ended with a pistol crack, but other memories still haunted her. She rose quickly, not wanting to follow those thoughts.

A glance in her mirror told her that she looked tolerably well, although, she decided, Jane's comment had been excessive. She indulged herself in a brief moment of pleasure that she had stood up for herself and not surrendered the cameo necklace to her acquisitive sister. It did go well with her gown.

Coming downstairs to the drawing room, she found Laura and Miss Parry already present and attended by Henry. He was wearing the regulation knee-breeches, and making disparaging comments about the hostesses, whom he liked no better than their father had.

Henry ceased conversing as he saw Tabitha and let out a long, low whistle. "Well, it was worth the wait, I think. You are in looks tonight, my dear. Indeed," he winked at Laura, "I might be escorting the beautiful Gunning sisters to the dance."

"Fie, Henry! Those low-born Irish wenches." Miss Parry sniffed.

Henry shook a finger at his aunt. "They were not Irish. They were Cornish. They were merely brought up in Ireland. And when they came to London to look for husbands one married the Duke of Hamilton and the other Lord Coventry. Remarkable, I'd say."

"Aye," his aunt said with a derisive smile, "Lady Coventry was the one who told George II that the sight she most wished to view was a coronation, not taking into account that His Majesty must needs die were he to oblige her."

"Must everyone prose on about people who died before I was born?" Laura complained. "Surely it is time for us to be leaving."

"Yes." Her brother grinned. "Do let us go and beard those three female dragons."

"Henry," his aunt reproved, "that is hardly the way to speak of Lady Jersey, the Countess de Lieven, and Mrs. Drummond-Burrell."

"Tell me another way and I will employ it." He laughed.

"Do let us go!" Laura prompted impatiently.

Henry's laugh grew louder. "So speaks Circe searching for victims to enchant."

"Oh, you." Laura made a face at him.

"Laura, your manners belong in the servants' hall," Miss Parry said sharply.

"Let her be, Aunt Ellen," Henry protested. "This is her evening, after all."

Miss Parry looked as if she might have more to say on the subject, but evidently thinking better of it, she said merely, "Very well, let us go."

Thanks to Laura's eagerness, they were among the first arrivals.

Laura, looking lovely in a celestial blue silk gown with little slippers to match and kid gloves to her elbows, was, as the patronesses demanded, amazingly subdued, her natural impetuosity in abeyance as her brother introduced her to the trio of gracious and extremely toplofty females he had stigmatized as dragon ladies: Mrs. Drummond-Burrell, the Countess de Lieven, and Lady Jersey. Laura, apparently aware that they had the power totally to blight her social career, was on her best behavior.

As they came away, Henry added in a whisper, "The countess is charm herself. She is particularly charming to statesmen and generals. She is, you must understand, a spy for her native Russia."

"A spy?" Laura exclaimed and received a quelling glance from her brother.

"Are you mad?" he muttered angrily, "I did not mean for you to bruit my comment over the whole ballroom."

"She did not," Tabitha assured him hastily. "I do not think anyone heard her. And I wonder, Henry, how you come by your information."

"But," Laura persisted in a lower voice, "why is she allowed to be here, if she steals state secrets?"

"She purloins only those she is meant to steal. She is far more informative than she believes and far less informed than she hopes. Now, on with the dance, let joy be unconfined, to quote from Lord Byron!"

Laura turned quickly to Tabitha. "I pray you will not be too weary sitting and chatting with Aunt Ellen." She indicated rows of small chairs with gilded backs and velvet cushions set back from the dancers and occupied by a number of young girls and elderly women.

"Oh, no," Tabitha assured her. "If I am not asked to dance, I shall still enjoy watching the dancers."

"Really?" Laura regarded her incredulously. "I should not like that at all."

"I am no prophet," Miss Parry murmured, "but I am sure neither of you will sit in the chairs for long, if at all, my dear Laura."

And, indeed, Miss Parry was correct. No sooner had the sisters appeared than both were surrounded by eager young men, all demanding introductions so that their names could be inserted in the little programs Laura and Tabitha carried.

There were so many requests that Laura, gazing at her completely filled program, murmured to Tabitha, "I vow, I'll not be able to tell one gentleman from another!"

"Nor I," Tabitha murmured and smothered a laugh as she met her sister's astonished look. She held up her program.

"Oh," Laura said, gazing at it in wonder. "And who asked for a waltz? I do wish I could waltz."

"That is a distinction that has to be earned." Tabitha laughed. "If you comport yourself appropriately, the patronesses might give you the nod quickly. But you must earn the permission. That would apply even if you married in your first Season."

"I wonder who it is I will marry," Laura murmured. "I wish it might be Henry's friend Lord Ashton, though he is rather old, but certainly he is the most handsome man

I have ever seen. And . . ." Her speculations ceased as a young man came to claim her for a cotillion at the same time Tabitha was escorted to the floor by another gentleman.

Some time later, after she had stood up for a cotillion, a country dance, a waltz, and another country dance, Tabitha, fanning herself, looked at her program. Another waltz was next. She tried to decipher the name she had written. Aster? Astor? There had been so many gentlemen surrounding her that she had been kept busy inserting their names in the appropriate places in her program without even looking up.

"My dance, I believe," said a familiar voice, and Tabitha looked up to find Lord Ashton standing before her.

"Oh," she murmured.

He looked rather confused. "It is my dance, I think?"

"It is, indeed, my lord. I . . . I had quite forgotten you had come into the title. And I so scribbled the name I couldn't read it. Pray forgive me."

"There is nothing to forgive, Lady Tabitha. I completely understand. You have been away so long."

There was an odd note in his voice. It sounded as if, indeed, he regretted the length of her absence. That, she assured herself, could be naught but a flight of fancy, for certainly his life in these past years had been very full.

"Come," he prompted. "The music has begun." He whirled her onto the floor.

They had danced together many times, but never the waltz. When first she had come to Almack's, the dance had not been permitted in its hallowed halls, she remembered. She was glad that it had finally found favor with the patronesses, even if a gentleman must still be careful not to hold his partner too closely.

She yielded herself to the music, and the light insistence of her partner. It was over all too soon, and he, leading her off the floor, smiled at her, saying hopefully, "Would there be another place for me upon that crowded program?"

She shook her head, managing not to sound as disappointed as she felt, as she said, "I fear there is not, my lord."

"That was my fear, Lady Tabitha. You are in such looks tonight and, as I remembered, grace itself upon the dance floor."

"You are kind to tell me so, my lord." She smiled up at him.

"No, I beg to differ with you. It was not kindness which prompted my remark, Lady Tabitha. I spoke the truth." He was gazing earnestly down at her, and she, meeting his eyes, felt as she had felt years ago when an unknown diffident youth had put his name down for a country dance and in the doing of it had claimed first her attention and then her heart.

"My lady," an eager voice was in her ear. "It is my dance, I believe."

"I must needs surrender you," her partner said reluctantly.

"I fear you must, my lord." She forced a smile and let the young man who was her new partner lead her onto the floor for a cotillion.

When the dance was ended, Tabitha scanned the floor for Lord Ashton. Her mind stumbled over the title. To her he was still Lord Lovell, but she must acclimate herself to his new honor. His words were still in her ears, and for a brief moment time had not existed.

"I do not believe that you sat out a single dance, Tabitha," Laura said as the three ladies were assisted into the waiting coach by Henry, who had been summoned from the card room. He was pleased to leave, he informed them, because he had been winning, and such luck, he had feared, could not last indefinitely.

Tabitha smiled. Her sister had sounded aggrieved, as if she resented Tabitha's success. Remembering Laura's earlier comments, she found herself uncommonly pleased to agree. "No, I did not, and nor did you, I think."

"Of course I wouldn't," Laura said loftily. She added, "I do hope you will not be too wearied by all your exertion to ride tomorrow morning?"

"Tomorrow morning?" Miss Parry echoed. "It is already tomorrow morning, for it is well past midnight." She yawned. "Neither of you should ride."

"I have every intention of so doing," Laura said, a shade defiantly. "I have always wanted to ride in the park."

"And I will be pleased to chaperone her." Tabitha smiled.

"I do not know where you get your energy," Miss Parry exclaimed. "But," she added in ominous accents, "we shall see how you are feeling tomorrow morning."

"I shall go, no matter how I feel," Laura replied.

= 4 =

"Is LAURA NOT DOWN yet?" Tabitha, dressed for riding, joined her aunt in the breakfast parlor. On a sideboard were various dishes under silver covers. The odor of coffee reached her. There was always tea and chocolate as well, but she preferred coffee.

Miss Parry regarded her with considerable amazement. "I vow, you have more energy than most of your family put together!"

"That, Aunt Ellen," Tabitha smiled, "is an exaggeration. You, too, have risen early. But it is a very long time since I have ridden in the park and I am looking forward to it. I wonder where Laura is?"

"She is awake. She came down, grumbling that Betsy had shaken her awake, but since it was at her orders, I don't think she has any cause for complaint," Miss Parry said, a slightly sour smile playing about her mouth. "She's gone upstairs again to rest until you are ready."

"Good heavens!" Tabitha exclaimed. "I thought Laura would be up, booted, spurred, and in the saddle long before I was ready to leave."

"One cannot have such a success as Laura enjoyed last night without its taking its toll—Good heavens!" Miss Parry stared at Tabitha.

"What is amiss?" Tabitha asked in some surprise.

"Nothing is amiss. I was thinking that you, too, enjoyed a similar success and she can give you nine years.

Yet here you are, ready to leave on a moment's notice and there she is, abed again."

Tabitha said kindly, "Laura is unused to such excitement. I had a taste of it before."

"All the same," Miss Parry began and paused as Laura, dressed for riding, entered slowly. "Good morning, my dear."

"Good . . . morning, Aunt Ellen." Laura yawned and without waiting for a response, turned amazed eyes on her sister. "You are here already?"

"As you see." Tabitha nodded. "I told you I would be ready to ride, and I am. Are you?"

"Of course," Laura snapped. "Did you imagine I would not be?"

"I imagined no such thing, my dear, since this ride was your notion, not mine," Tabitha responded. "Come . . . have your breakfast and let us go."

Watching her sister as she drooped over the breakfast table, Tabitha was surprised at her sister's eagerness to ride, when it was obvious that she would have been the better for a few more hours of sleep. Still, the lure of the park for one who had never ridden there was understandable. It was wonderful to be able to ride in the heart of a great city. She suddenly, unwillingly remembered a race (a strictly forbidden activity) with a young Lord Lovell. He had teased her and said he would not give her a handicap and she—

She choked off the memory. She did not want to dwell on that or on the excitement she had experienced the previous night when they had gone through the once forbidden paces of the waltz. Perhaps it were best if it were still forbidden, she thought unhappily.

She looked up as one of the footmen entered the breakfast parlor. "Your ladyships' horses are here," he announced.

"Thank you, Thomas," said Tabitha with relief, glad to be rid of her intrusive memories.

"I vow," Laura remarked in a bantering tone, "you were more than half asleep."

"On the contrary," Tabitha said coolly. "I was thinking."

"Of your great success last night, perchance?"

"Not really," Tabitha said lightly. There had been an edge to Laura's voice as if, indeed, she had been irked by that same success.

She was sure of it when Laura added, "I wish those old cats would give me permission to waltz at Almack's."

"They won't be in a hurry to do so if you continue to refer to them in that manner," said Tabitha repressively.

In a matter of a few minutes, they were mounted: Tabitha on Mark, a handsome chestnut gelding, and Laura on Queen Anne, or Annie, as she called her mare. The horses were eager to break into a canter but had to be restrained as the sisters worked their way along Upper Grosvenor Street to Park Lane, and thence to the park entrance.

As they reached the great gates, Tabitha noted that Laura was drooping in her saddle.

But then, as they progressed farther, Laura suddenly said, "I want to gallop. You wait here and keep a look out."

"A look out for what?"

"For other people. It is forbidden to gallop here. You were the one who told me. I just want to run—oh, as far as the tree nearest the Serpentine."

"I don't see how I can warn you if someone does approach," Tabitha said. "But I don't see anyone about. Let's race! On the count of three."

"No," shouted Laura.

But Tabitha was already counting. As she reached three, she gave Mark his head. A quick backward look showed her Laura was using her whip viciously. She started to protest but quickly changed her mind. Laura would not take kindly to a reprimand. Her little sister was in a decidedly edgy mood already.

Urging her own horse forward and feeling the cool morning breeze against her face, she was glad Laura had suggested the ride. It was singularly pleasant to be out at this early hour, and racing, too, was exhilarating. She loved the feel of the wind in her face.

She wondered if she should have given Laura a handicap and then decided that it was probably as well she hadn't. Her sister might resent it as a slur on her riding. She was always quick to take offense even when none was intended. With a small sigh, Tabitha rode forward, her eyes on the goal.

They were nearing the designated tree, and though Tabitha had anticipated that Laura would be neck and neck with her by now, a quick glance backward showed her that Laura was still several lengths behind her and their groom almost out of sight. Laura was again using her whip violently. A protest rose to Tabitha's lips, but again she did not voice it, determinedly riding forward and reaching the goal in a few minutes.

Turning back, she saw Laura coming up behind her, but she noticed with some surprise, tugging futilely at her reins in an unavailing effort to halt Annie. To Tabitha's horror, Laura's mount galloped on quite out of control. Reaching the banks of the Serpentine, the horse came to an abrupt stop, tossing Laura over its head into the water. With a loud neigh, Annie galloped away to the accompaniment of Laura's desperate scream.

Hastily dismounting, Tabitha hurried toward the stream only to see a young man suddenly appear and plunge into the water. In another moment, he had his arm around a choking, gasping Laura and was wading with her to the bank. As Tabitha knelt to extend him a hand, she was aware of other riders coming up fast behind her. A quick glance showed her that one of them was Lord Ashton.

Obviously, he had summed up the situation, for, leaping off his horse and thrusting his reins to another man, who had also dismounted, he hurried to Tabitha's side. "Move back," he said quickly. "I will help her out."

As Tabitha obeyed, he knelt to receive the weeping, shivering girl from her rescuer's arms. Pulling her up on the bank, he hastily divested himself of his coat and wrapped it around Laura. Her rescuer followed, easily hoisting himself up on the bank. To Tabitha's astonishment, it was Frederick Perdue. "She must be taken home immediately," he said. "The water's cold. She could catch her death."

"No matter, Sir Frederick," Lord Ashton said. "My carriage is here. I'll see she and her sister are brought home and you, sir, must get a change of clothing and quickly. May I take you to your lodgings?"

"No, I . . . I thank you, my lord, I live not too far distant. I will leave Lady Laura in your hands." With a nod to Tabitha, he started to walk away.

"Sir Frederick," Tabitha called, but he seemed not to hear her, and in another moment he had disappeared among the trees.

"Oh, gracious, what a surprise," Tabitha said in some distress. "Are you all right, Laura?"

"Oh, yes," the girl said.

"I should not repine," Lord Ashton said coolly. "Are you acquainted with him?"

"Yes. No. That is . . . we, I, met him once many years ago . . . but only once—"

Lord Ashton broke into Laura's fractured speech, saying curtly, "Sir Frederick Perdue's reputation is none too savory. He has been called an ivory-turner, and he is a known Captain Sharp."

"Oh, dear, I wonder how he happened to be here?" Tabitha frowned, very much aware that his arrival had been far too fortuitous.

"He was at Almack's last night," Lord Ashton said. "I saw her standing up with him in one of the country dances. At first I thought it was you; your coloring is very similar to that of Lady Laura."

"P—please," Laura moaned. "I . . . I want to go home."

"Yes, of course, my dear, we will go at once. Lord Ashton has kindly offered us the use of his coach."

"And before she develops a quinsy, I think we must leave," Lord Ashton said.

"Of course," Tabitha agreed. "But our horses—and Laura's has run away."

"It will probably return to the stables, and your groom will see that yours is brought there, too." He motioned to where the man was standing with a sheepish look on his face, holding Tabitha's horse.

"Come, then." Lord Ashton lifted Laura in his arms, carrying her with an ease that surprised Tabitha. In a few moments, they had reached his coach, and a short time later they were home.

Once inside the house and explaining the circumstances to their bemused aunt, Tabitha could only marvel, remembering the way Lord Ashton had taken charge of her sobbing, hysterical sister, soothing her gently and actually managing to calm her down. He had wrapped her in the carriage blanket he had in his coach and had carried her into the house. Afterward, at the direction of a bemused Miss Parry, he had taken her up the stairs to her chamber, leaving her to the ministrations of her startled abigail.

As she accompanied him to the front door, Tabitha said warmly, "I do not know how to thank you, my lord. We would have been in sore straits without your help."

"You need not thank me, Lady Tabitha," he said. "Anyone would have done the same." His eyes lingered on her face. "I do hope your sister will not suffer any ill effects from her plunge into the Serpentine."

"So do I. Usually, she has excellent control of her mounts, but I think she was weary. She did not sit out a single dance last night."

"Nor did you," he said just a shade ruefully.

Tabitha found her heart pounding somewhere in the vicinity of her throat. She did not quite know how to respond to this comment. "I expect," she said lightly, after a moment's hesitation, "that new faces are always sought after."

"And I expect that the reason is quite, quite different." He smiled. "But," he added quickly, "I must go."

"Oh, yes, you must!" she cried, belatedly aware that there were large wet patches on his garments. "You might catch a quinsy, yourself."

"I truly doubt that, Lady Tabitha. I am made of much sterner stuff." He bent to kiss her hand.

"Fare you well," she said rather breathlessly. "I do thank you for your help."

"I am glad that I was present to be of service, Lady Tabitha." Turning, he hurried through the door which the wooden-faced footman held open for him.

Tabitha slowly mounted the stairs to the upper hall, meeting Miss Parry hurrying down. "Has Lord Ashton departed?" her aunt inquired.

"He has just gone," Tabitha said.

"Oh, dear, I am so very sorry I had not the chance to thank him for bringing Laura home so quickly. What a mercy he was present."

"Yes, a most fortunate coincidence, indeed," Tabitha agreed. "I remember that he always used to like early morning rides. He once asked me if I might accompany him, but Papa would not allow it." Tabitha smiled a little ruefully at the recollection.

"No, of course, he would not, my dear. I remember the incident, too, and you weeping and stamping your foot."

"Did I?" Tabitha regarded her in surprise.

"Oh, yes, you had quite a little temper in those days, my love, and you were given to passionate avowals such as 'if so and so does not happen, I will never be happy again.'"

"Really? I do not remember," Tabitha said. "Oh, dear, I must have been just like Laura."

"Not really, my dear," Miss Parry shook her head. "You never practiced duplicity. You were merely passionate."

"Was I? It seems like such a long time ago," Tabitha sighed.

"It does, does it not? But more to the point"—Miss Parry gave her a narrow look—"how did Laura happen to plunge into the Serpentine?"

"I suggested a race, but she was too weary to control her horse."

"Oh, dear, oh, dear." Miss Parry sighed. "I hope she does not catch cold. She is subject to them, as you know."

"She was not in the water very long."

"But the morning is cool and she was in her wet garments far too long. How ridiculous to rise at that hour. She was almost too weary to lift her head when she left." Miss Parry gave Tabitha a piercing look. "You are certain she did not have an ulterior motive?"

"No, she merely overestimated her strength," Tabitha said carefully, not wanting to get her sister in further trouble. There was no need to mention Sir Frederick. Most likely he had been there by chance. However, she must, she decided, watch Laura more closely. Meanwhile, she thought with a surge of pleasure, she would have this day to herself. She would look in on Laura and then visit Montague House, where the British Museum was located. It was an excursion she had planned years ago, she remembered sadly. Her father had promised to take her there but had been denied the opportunity to fulfill his promise.

"We are inclined to be forgetful of how very much London offers, my love," he had said. "In addition to the treasures of the antiquity, there are the fascinating artifacts gathered by Captain Cook on his voyages to New South Wales and to the Hawaiian Islands." He had sighed. "Poor man, dead and only fifty-one. Killed by a cannibal king."

Tabitha had a sigh for her father, slain at the age of forty-three by a young man who, for that moment, had been no less savage. She grimaced and wished that memory would not keep furnishing images of the past, for following them came other, more recent images. Engraved on her inner vision was the scene they had encountered in this very house. Henry and his mistress and the slender, beautiful dancer who had gaped at her lover with her heart in her eyes. Had her father's opera dancer gazed at him with the adoration Lord Ashton commanded?

The two men should not be compared, protested part of her mind. Her father had suffered no devastating loss. It was his family that had suffered. She, herself, had endured a double loss, for who knew what might have happened had her acquaintance with Lord Ashton ripened and deepened?

A sigh escaped her and she shook her head. It did no good to dwell on such possibilities. Had she been a fool in rejecting all the proposals that came her way after her period of mourning was at the end? Probably, but she had found no one for whom she cared as much as she had cared for the young man she had known for so brief a time. Why were these thoughts assailing her mind at this moment? Perhaps it was her thought of the British Museum and its association in her mind with her father, and the subsequent memories this had engendered.

She would think only of the British Museum. She would go immediately. It was an ideal time to see it. Laura was in bed, and later, when the girl recovered from her experience, Tabitha would be too busy shepherding her sister about to think about her own wants.

"No, not by yourself." Miss Parry, informed of her niece's decision, frowned. "You must wait until your sister is better and I am not administering to her."

"Nonsense," Tabitha replied calmly. "I remember from years ago that you did not wish to visit the museum, and I cannot believe that you are any more interested in it at present. And wild horses would not be able to drag Laura there, I am certain. I will go this morning and save you both the horrid necessity of accompanying me."

"You should not go alone." Miss Parry frowned. "You are too good-looking a young woman to go anywhere unchaperoned. There are far too many gentlemen on the lookout for unescorted females."

"Females of mature years, Aunt Ellen?" Tabitha demanded with an edge of sarcasm to her tone.

"You do not wear your accumulation of years on your forehead, Tabitha, my dear."

"Are you willing to accompany me to the museum at such a time as Laura is better? Tramping up and down stairs to look at artifacts from Greece and Rome, sarcophagi from Egypt, and strange idols from the South Seas and Hawaii?"

Tabitha laughed as an involuntary grimace twisted Miss Parry's mouth. She said, gaily, "There, I have your answer written large on your face! I shall be back to relieve you at Laura's bedside and keep her amused, for I doubt she makes a quiet patient. Meanwhile, I shall have seen Alexander's tomb and the Rosetta Stone. Oh, I do wish you could see your face, Aunt Ellen. I will go alone and thus save you the suffering you would undoubtedly endure."

"Your abigail," murmured her aunt weakly.

"Jane is much too busy, and her feet hurt if she has to walk too much."

"Very well," her aunt said reluctantly. "Since there is no talking you out of this unfortunate venture, do as you choose. But please take the coach and have Bartlett wait for you."

"I will, of course, Aunt Ellen," Tabitha said, managing with some effort to suppress a smile which reflected both amusement and pleasure.

= 5 =

WHEN THEY HAD FINALLY driven to Bloomsbury, some distance from the house, and the coachman had stopped twice to ask directions, they reached the British Museum. Tabitha felt a real thrill of anticipation as she gazed up at the massive outlines of the building.

It was pleasant for Tabitha to know that one could wait nine years for an anticipated treat, and—when one finally had the opportunity to enjoy it—still not be too old for the pleasure. She remembered being Laura's age, and facing the idea of one day being twenty with some displeasure and trepidation. At that time she had thought that twenty-five would bring the onset of old age!

The footman opened the door for her, and she descended to find the coachman turning on the box to catch her attention. " 'Adn't Timothy," he indicated the footman, "better go in wi' you, yer ladyship?" he asked.

With a smile, she said, "Certainly not, Bartlett. I am sure he would find it monstrous dull."

A swift glance at the footman corroborated her comment. There had been just a hint of sulkiness in his carefully schooled features when Bartlett made his proposal. Immediately after she voiced her opinion, however, he grinned in a most relieved manner, then quickly remembered his place and once again assumed the attentive but disinterested look he had been trained in.

Turning again to the coachman, she said, "I will not be overlong, Bartlett."

"Yes, yer ladyship." He nodded dutifully while gazing at her rather anxiously. "Timothy an' I, we'll be right here for yer ladyship."

That her coachman's views had unwittingly coincided with her aunt's views both annoyed her and amused her. They spoke as if she were a green girl rather than a mature female of twenty-seven. She was hardly in need of a chaperone. A chaperone for a chaperone? The idea was ridiculous!

"Is there an inn nearby?" Tabitha asked, her mind firmly made up that the servants were not going to wait patiently for her in the street.

"Yes, yer ladyship," Bartlett replied doubtfully. "I drove past a house called the Duck and Drake, no more than three streets down."

"Well," said Tabitha, "I expect I'll spend a couple of hours in the museum. You and Timothy can wait there. Bring the carriage here just before noon."

She opened her reticule and took out a few coins. "Here," she added, passing Bartlett the coins, "it should pay for the stabling of the horses, and let you and Timothy have a pint."

"Thank you, yer ladyship, but are you sure that's all right? I could always drive back to the house and then come back here for you again."

Tabitha saw no point in that. Her aunt would undoubtedly scold Bartlett for leaving her. "No, I'd rather you waited at the Duck and Drake." She laughed, knowing that Bartlett always liked a simple joke. "But don't run up too big a tab. I only have ten pounds with me!" she called gaily over her shoulder as she walked toward the museum.

Considerably pleased that she had been able to impose her will on the coachman and, in essence, on Miss Parry, and also pleased that she had finally arrived at a building she had longed to visit some nine years earlier, Tabitha happily mounted the steps of Montague House.

It had once been the home of the late Duke of Montague and, she remembered, purchased in 1754 to house various collections deeded to the government and ranging in scope from Grecian and Egyptian antiquities to coins and books from two notable collections.

In the ensuing sixty-odd years a great many more treasures had been deeded to the museum, some of which had been captured during the Napoleonic Wars. Among these was the Rosetta Stone, with its three inscriptions in Egyptian hieroglyphics, in demotic script, and in Greek. Her father had told her that some scholars believed the carving on the Rosetta Stone to contain the key to the Egyptian language. The stone itself and other Egyptian relics stood in sheds outside the museum.

She spent several minutes carefully looking at the great green sarcophagus, said to be the tomb of Alexander the Great. She was fascinated by it, but it was a warm morning and she much preferred to go inside into the shade.

No doubt, Tabitha thought as she entered the great hall of the museum, the late Duke of Montague would have been extremely surprised and possibly angered to discover that the vast space where once he had welcomed his guests was now given over to the exhibits that thronged the floors.

If, as she strongly doubted, there were ghosts, she could imagine their spectral selves confusedly drifting around, or rather through, huge black marble statues supposedly removed from the tomb of Cleopatra, or staring with amazement at a great, strangely carved ram's head nearby.

Opposite the stairs that stretched to the second floor was a model of the Blackfriars Bridge, appearing even more incongruous when one looked up at the gold-leafed and painted ceilings dating from the days of the duke. Tabitha smiled at her mental image of the ghost looking down, muttering, "What, what, what?"

After signing her name in the register, Tabitha, going toward the stairs leading to the first floor, was surprised at the paucity of visitors to the museum. She doubted that there were more than twenty or thirty people on the ground floor, and a glance at the first floor convinced her that it was even less crowded.

She found herself singularly pleased at that. She would be spared the inevitable speculations regarding the so-called origins of the various artifacts, delivered, her father had once said contemptuously, by know-nothings masquerading as know-everythings.

Having mounted the stairs to the first floor, Tabitha entered a chamber containing cases displaying Egyptian funerary jars topped by heads of Toth, Isis, and Set. These failed to hold her interest long, and as she started out of the room she nearly collided with a young man accompanied by an elderly woman. The woman uttered a little cry of fright as her companion pulled up short.

"I do hope you were not hurt," the woman said in a soft, cultured tone of voice. "My son," she had a reproving glance for the young man, "has an unfortunate habit of never watching where he is going. Perhaps you should come and sit down for a moment. It must have been a nasty shock."

"That is quite all right," Tabitha assured her hastily, stepping around her. "I was not harmed." With a brief smile, and before the woman, who had started to put a solicitous hand on her arm, could complete her gesture, she hurried out of the chamber. She had no desire to fall into conversation with the woman. She was in no mood to converse, particularly with strangers. She wanted to be alone.

It was singularly pleasant to be away from Laura, who was certain to be in a vile humor after her plunge into the stream. While Tabitha doubted that Laura would suffer any embarrassment by the unlooked for and surprising reappearance of Sir Frederick Perdue, she would undoubtedly be on the defensive. Even if Tabitha did not broach the topic, Laura would try to batter down her sister's unvoiced suspicions that Laura had made an assignation with him. But even Laura must have been aware that a meeting in the park with Tabitha and a groom in attendance would have been impossible.

Tabitha was not being entirely frank with herself. There was another subject she did not wish to discuss with Laura. There had been another fortuitous appearance, one Tabitha knew was not contrived, that of Lord Ashton.

As usual, Tabitha found herself divided on the topic of Lord Ashton. Her heart wanted to savor the brief meeting in silence; her mind wanted distraction from it. And so she was killing two birds with one stone, in visiting the museum.

She loosed a long sigh, wondering when her heart would cease to beat faster each time she so much as glimpsed him. Indeed, this morning she had felt much as she had when first she met him and had seen interest flare in his eyes. But in those days she had been young, and while she had in essence remained faithful to her memories of him, unable even to think of another man, he had loved and lost his wife.

She shuddered. She was spoiling her visit to the museum. It was ridiculous to dwell on the recent past when she could divert herself among the remains of more ancient eras, and even more ridiculous to feel her heart beat faster as she had earlier this morning when Lord Ashton had suddenly appeared in the park. It was time she realized that she was caught in an old dream, one that had lasted far too long.

Resolutely, she turned into another chamber, this one containing garish masks and long shields painted with odd designs. Evidently, she had found the collection of poor Captain Cook. She shuddered as her eyes fell on a small, exceedingly ugly idol. There was something peculiarly evil in its carved countenance.

"Ah, my dear, here you are. You should never wander off by yourself, not in these rooms." Someone had put a hand on her left arm.

Startled, Tabitha turned to see the elderly lady she had encountered as she came out of the Egyptian collection.

Then, as she recognized her, the young man stepped to her other side, grasping her right arm.

Incredulously, she looked from one to the other. "Might I ask the meaning of this?" she demanded coldly. "You will please release me. I am not in need of your protection. Indeed, I consider it an unwarranted familiarity!" She tried to pull away, and to her amazement, their grips tightened.

"Then, dearie, let us have your ten pounds," the woman demanded.

"Ten pounds? What ever makes you think I have ten pounds?" Tabitha asked, trying to keep the fright from her voice while she struggled to free herself.

"Now, now, lamb, I heard you calling out to your coachman, as bold as brass. Come, come, hand it over, or it will go hard with you, I fear."

"But I don't have it." Of course she wouldn't have so much money on her. Bartlett had known it was a joke, but apparently this woman didn't. Tabitha managed to pull her arm free from the woman, but the young man was still holding her tightly. She found it almost impossible to believe that she was being robbed in broad daylight, and in a public place.

The old woman grabbed Tabitha's reticule and opened it. She took out a couple of coins and Tabitha's handkerchief. She slipped the coins into her own capacious reticule and rubbed the hem of the handkerchief between her thumb and forefinger. "Nice bit of material," she remarked.

Fear bubbled in Tabitha's throat, and with it anger. "Let go of me, you insolent creatures! You have taken my money, now let me go!"

"You will not raise your voice again, dearie," the woman warned. She seized Tabitha's arm again and said to her son, "You'd better stick her."

Tabitha felt something small and pointed against her ribs. It had to be a knife! She sent a frantic look about the room, hoping against hope that there was someone else in the far reaches of the chamber or even passing by outside in the corridor. There had to be people about, people somewhere in the museum, but at present there was no one.

Still, she repeated, shouting in hopes that she'd be heard, "Let me go!" Her voice echoed in the room.

There were no answering shouts promising help.

"That was very foolish, dearie," said the woman softly. And at the same time Tabitha felt a searing pain along her rib. She gasped.

The woman's hold on her arm tightened. "Where is the money?"

Tabitha thought desperately. Perhaps downstairs there would be someone to help her. "I left it in the coach. Do let me go."

"Then we will all go there. The Duck and Drake, you said. And, lamb, I do hope you haven't hidden the money about yourself, for my son would be happy to look for it." The old woman spoke matter-of-factly, but her son grinned in a most unpleasant way.

He hadn't spoken once, and Tabitha concluded that his mother was the mastermind of their most unpleasant little family business.

She didn't reply to the woman's threat. When they reached the inn, Bartlett and Timothy would be there to help her. And she would beg assistance of anyone they passed.

As they left the room, an old man entered. At once, Tabitha said, "Sir, please, sir." She felt again the bite of the knife.

"My niece," the old woman said smoothly, "has been badly frightened by these exhibits, those bones, and the nasty mummies, too."

The old man shook his head and chuckled. "You ought not to be afraid of them, young lady. They are all dead and gone these thousand years or more."

"Come, dearest, we will leave this horrid place," the woman said. Smiling at Tabitha, she added, "Hurry, my love, you'll feel better once you're home."

The elderly man was too frail to overcome her assailants. The fear of being stabbed again to no purpose and seeing the old man harmed kept Tabitha silent. With the sharp and threatening prodding of the knife in her ribs, Tabitha walked through the exhibition room as slowly as she dared, but the woman's tug on her arm kept urging her to come quickly.

She had no recourse but to obey, loathing the hard clasp of the woman's hand on her arm, and the lighter, but more deadly touch of her son and his knife. Tabitha was beginning to be afraid that they would encounter no one who could offer assistance. The thieves would take her directly to the inn yard, search the carriage and her before anyone noticed—and then? Perhaps in their rage they would kill her.

She vowed to herself that if she saw anyone who could swiftly release her from the thieves, she would call out again. Even if she met no one on this floor who could help her, once they were downstairs, there had to be someone, someone strong enough to give her assistance. She would call out even if there was no one in sight.

However much the man and his knife might hurt her, there was less chance of her being killed if there were more witnesses than he could overpower. She was certain that on the more crowded lower floor there were some people who would hear her and come running.

And then she saw Lord Ashton at the foot of the stairs. "Lionel!" she cried, unaware that she used his given name—a name she had never permitted herself to use, even in her mind. "Lionel! Help me!"

She gasped as the knife snaked along her side. Lord Ashton paused not even for a second, but was up the steps three at a time. He struck the man at her side full in the face. With a cry, her male captor released her and lunged forward. Lord Ashton grabbed him and flung him down the staircase. He rolled down the steps to lie still at the bottom.

The old woman dropped Tabitha's arm and fled screaming down the stairs. "My son, my son, you killed my boy."

Tabitha sank down weakly, sitting on the top step, resting her head against the railings.

The next half hour was a blur: Lord Ashton asking if she were all right . . . the kindly lady with hartshorn . . . the sip of brandy from a gentleman's flask . . . the arrest of the woman and her injured son . . . her hesitant explanation of the jest about the ten pounds . . . the babble of voices . . . the ringing in her ears.

And then Lord Ashton was by her side. "Thank God Lady Laura left her crop in my carriage. I found it halfway home and turned about to return it. Miss Parry told me you'd come here. I thought I'd see if you wanted company on your visit."

"I was such a fool. Aunt Ellen warned me not to come alone."

"I hardly think she expected you to be robbed."

"No," said Tabitha. "She just worries. Would you help me up, please?"

Lord Ashton assisted her to her feet. "My carriage is outside."

"I sent Bartlett and Timothy to wait until noon at the Duck and Drake. . . ."

"I will have a message sent. I'll take you home. There's no reason for you to have to wait." Firmly and politely brushing aside offers of assistance from others, he took Tabitha, who was leaning heavily on his arm, out of the museum and helped her into his carriage.

As she sat down, her cloak fell open. "What is this?" Lord Ashton pulled the garment away from her side. "Your gown is soaked in blood."

"He had—he had . . . a knife," Tabitha said. "It's nothing . . . nothing." She was starting to shake.

"It is not nothing." Lord Ashton pulled off his neckcloth and made it into a pad. "Press this to your side," he said, wrapping her cloak about her. "And lie down." He lifted her legs onto the seat.

She tried to protest, then decided it wasn't worth it. "It doesn't hurt."

"I'm afraid it will soon. Your courage is to be commended—oh, my dear, do not weep." Suddenly he was sitting beside her, and she was propped against his chest, his arms around her.

"I was so very frightened."

"And so very brave."

= 6 =

DR. CLARKE, A PHYSICIAN Lord Ashton recommended, was brought to Tabitha's bedside. He found her wounds no more than superficial and, at his orders, Jane put a poultice on them. The doctor advised Tabitha to remain in bed for the rest of the day but said that she could get up the next day if she wished. "Trust to your own good sense not to tire yourself."

"I don't feel as though I have much good sense," Tabitha said. "My aunt warned me not to go to the British Museum alone."

"Lady Tabitha, do you wish me to express my opinion of your visit to the museum?"

"I can imagine what it is, sir."

"Indeed? I think that you could not have known what would have happened to you. You are a capable woman, Lady Tabitha, obviously not given to hysterics. I think you would have been well about to deal with the danger Miss Parry imagined—encroaching men. And I think you dealt very well with the danger you encountered. One can expect pickpockets in public places, but not knife-wielding brigands."

Despite the doctor's words, Tabitha still felt very foolish, for her silly remark about the ten pounds had had very unpleasant consequences. After Dr. Clarke had taken his leave, she sat in bed sipping a strong cup of tea, trying to collect her thoughts. It had been such an eventful day already, and it was only just after noon.

Thank goodness Lord Ashton had arrived when he did. But despite his kindness to her on the drive home, she strongly feared she must have fallen in his esteem as well. Ironically, as soon as he had praised her courage, she had been unable to restrain her tears.

Oh, why couldn't she stop caring what he thought about her? It ought to be enough that he had very likely saved her life, or at least prevented her from being very badly hurt.

In the midst of these unhappy reflections, Miss Parry came into the room. She went to the foot of Tabitha's bed, and intoned, "Twice in one day. Twice!" she repeated. "Lord Ashton has rescued the pair of you! It is too much to ask, even of a knight-errant. I warned you not to go to the museum alone, and I thank God Lord Ashton agreed with me!"

"He told you that?" Tabitha sighed. Had everyone but she expected armed robbers there?

"No, but obviously he agreed, for why else would he have gone to keep you company? You cannot say I did not do my very best to dissuade you." Miss Parry shook her head. "I do thank God for Lord Ashton. Had he not come this morning, you might . . . you might have been . . ." Tears stood in her eyes. "Those foul, horrible miscreants, to use you so! Does your side still hurt?"

It did hurt and throb, but Tabitha shook her head. "They were not very deep cuts," she said.

"That they should have touched you, let alone hurt you," Miss Parry said furiously. "But enough, my dear, try and sleep. It is 'chief nourisher in life's feast,' says Shakespeare. Shall I sit with you?"

"No, thank you, Aunt Ellen. I expect that you are busy enough with Laura."

"I have not told her yet. I do not want her fretting, for I think she is coming down with a cold."

Much to Tabitha's surprise, her aunt, who was never demonstrative, bent and kissed her on her cheek. "I do not know what I should have done," she said chokingly and hurried from the chamber, closing the door softly behind her.

Tabitha ordered Jane to open the curtains, for she still felt too overwrought to sleep, then dismissed her abigail. She lay staring up at the window.

The sun was bright and the sky a cerulean blue. Who would have thought that on such a day . . . ? She shuddered, seeing in her mind's eye the two people who had accosted her. She did not think she would ever forget the faces of the woman and her silent son, the feel of the hands on her arms, the horrid anticipation of the stab of the knife, which was much worse than the actual cut. She would always remember the anxious relief that she did not feel the wound, and the sickening thought that the next stab might be the last thing she ever felt.

Perhaps she should try to find escape in sleep. Although she hesitated to seem so vacillating, she rang for Jane and requested that the curtains be drawn. Then, to calm herself, she recalled her rescue. Lord Ashton's dash up the stairs to her side, the blow with which he overcame her attacker; the feeling of freedom as her arms were released.

Tabitha reached behind her head and adjusted a pillow slightly. The walk on Lord Ashton's arm to his carriage, the relief as the carriage pulled away from the museum, Lord Ashton's concern and anger when he realized she was injured, his care in helping her lie down, the feel of his arms about her . . . Tabitha fell into an exhausted sleep.

Late in the afternoon, Tabitha awoke to find a bouquet of beautiful roses in a crystal vase on the table by her bed. There was a small envelope below it on which her name was written in a flowing script.

With fingers that were not quite steady, she opened it to find a note reading:

> My Dear Lady Tabitha:
> If you have recuperated from your visit to the
> British Museum by Friday, may I hope that you

will wish to join my sister Katherine, Lady Lydford and me for a gentle ride in the park? If you will do me the honor, there is no need to answer this note. My sister and I will be at your house by eleven in the morning.

I remain your servant,
Ashton.

Friday was four days distant. Of course, she would be recovered by then, Tabitha thought. In fact, she was feeling better already! Her sleep had improved her spirits marvelously.

No, her spirits owed that improvement to this small sheet of crested paper which she had read twice already, and would read again and again.

No, she said sharply to herself. It was the sleep. And she would most certainly not read the note again. But she would ride with Lord Ashton and his sister, just to prove that she could be in his company without her foolish heart bleating like a silly sheep's.

After a quiet week during which Tabitha excused herself from evening entertainment in the earlier part, Friday morning arrived. Tabitha, clad in a blue riding habit only a shade lighter than her dark blue eyes, came to stand at the foot of Laura's bed, sent there by a harried Miss Parry, who had told her that her sister was in a rare taking.

"Well," she said, coolly meeting Laura's angry stare. "What's amiss?"

"You are leaving me with Aunt Ellen for the fourth day in a row." Laura glared at her accusingly. "I hardly glimpsed you yesterday—you were too busy calling on all the ladies whose routs and balls and whatnot we could not attend because I was ill and you were still recovering. And what do I hear this morning? You are going riding. If I'd gotten myself into such a scrape as you did on Monday, I should have been house-bound for a week at the very least!"

"That is the difference between youth and age,"

Tabitha said lightly. "And if we are going to discuss scrapes, my dear, it was your plunge into the Serpentine that brought you to this pass." Since Miss Parry was not present, she decided to broach the topic. "And I pray you'll not tell me that Sir Frederick Perdue appeared out of nowhere quite by accident."

"That is what I do tell you!" Laura cried. "I had no notion that he was there. It had nothing to do with me, I vow." She sneezed.

"Well," Tabitha said, "how fortunate that he was present to rescue you."

"And how fortunate Lord Ashton was on hand to rescue you," Laura retorted. Her eyes narrowed. "Or did you expect to meet him at the museum?"

"Laura, you are becoming impertinent. I went to see the treasures of the ancient world," Tabitha said coldly. "You see, I do not happen to possess your inherent deviousness. Now, if you will excuse me. . . ." She walked quickly out of her sister's chamber and only by a strong exercise of will did she refrain from slamming the door.

She did stand against it for a moment, for she needed to calm down. Not for the first time, she strongly regretted the need for constant supervision of her sister. If only she had been stricter with Laura when she was a child.

Tabitha, her siblings, and even their aunt, had been wont to make a pet of the motherless child, fussing over her and giving in to her demands for attention. But they felt too sorry for her to punish her when her demands went beyond what was proper and polite. Henry in particular had encouraged her to misbehave and make precocious and often vulgar speeches.

Tabitha wondered if much of Laura's outrageous behavior, now obviously merely a bad habit, had begun as a way of keeping her older sister and her aunt focused on her as she lost her parents to death and her older siblings to marriage.

It was a blessing that James was a boy and only two years older than Laura. He had been at Eton, and so had missed the fond attention that had so spoiled Laura. To borrow a phrase from her aunt, Tabitha did not think she could cope with another young lady of Laura's temperament.

Tabitha was hopeful that she would have some two or three more days of surcease until Laura recovered completely. She frowned, wondering how many Sir Fredericks would be slyly awaiting her. Indeed, she did not need to be a prophet to predict the spate of trouble in which Laura would be involved and in which she, very possibly, would have to share. The girl, alas, had never profited by experience. She frowned. Why dwell on that? Think instead of this morning's ride and the fact that for a short time she would be herself, not Laura's middle-aged chaperone! If only . . . but there was no use dwelling on that cruelly aborted friendship of nine years past, nor did she dare mistake kindness for interest. Her aunt had pointed that out and she agreed. She really ought not to resent the presence of Laura, either, for were it not for the need to present her to Society, they would still be in Derbyshire.

It was lovely to be riding in the park, lovely to ride with Lord Ashton and his sister. Tabitha had imagined that she was younger than her brother, but she proved to be a good many years older than he. At the time of Tabitha's Season, Katherine was a year married to Lord Lydford, and had spent that spring at York in the company of the dowager Lady Lydford. But she was a tiny woman, and Tabitha saw why Lord Ashton called her his little sister.

"I'm sorry you won't meet my husband," she told Tabitha after they were introduced. "He is in Canada. Something to do with building a military canal." Lady Lydford rolled eyes of a translucent green only a shade lighter than those of her brother.

"The Military Canal," corrected her brother. "To move supplies and troops in case the Americans try to invade," he explained.

She sighed. "I understand that is in the wilds of Ontario." Lord Ashton chuckled. "My love, as I believe I have often told you, there is nothing wild about that part of Ontario. It is well-populated and fast becoming a civilized part of the world from what I hear, but you will persist in imagining that Lydford is in immediate danger of being attacked by Indians! Do allow me to reassure you that they have learned to avoid such areas."

Lady Lydford pulled a face. "I do hope my dear husband will not be so enamored of it to insist that we settle there."

"Lydford leave England?" Lord Ashton chuckled. "I do doubt it very strongly, my dear." Turning to Tabitha, he added, "This fair English rose has a will of iron and is determined only to bloom in English soil. I imagine that you must be in agreement with her?"

"I am, though I should not mind visiting Canada and other parts of the American continent."

"Now there's bravery." He smiled warmly, and suddenly Tabitha was wafted back in time to the ballroom at Almack's and the young man whose name was on her program for a dance and with whom she had fallen in love between one moment and the next. Much about him had changed, but that smile, that lovely smile, remained the same.

"I imagine—" she began and then emitted a startled little cry, as there was a pounding of hooves behind them. In another moment, a lone horseman had passed them, riding perilously close to their party as he stared at Tabitha out of hard amber eyes.

Lady Lydford's horse shied violently and might have unseated her had it not been for her brother's hasty grasp of her reins and his soothing murmurs to her fractious mount.

"What the devil," he said explosively. "Who was that madman? I do wish I had been able to get a closer look at him!" He looked toward Tabitha, whose horse, also restive, was calming down as she alternately patted him and murmured soothing words to him. "I would like to teach him manners with a whip!"

"L-Lion, I . . . I think I . . . I really must return to . . . to the s-stables. You do understand. I . . . I cannot afford to . . . to take chances at this time," Lady Lydford said faintly. "If anything happens to me, the children will be alone for months before . . . before their father returns."

"My love, are you all right?" her brother asked anxiously.

"Yes, but . . ."

"We will go back, of course."

"Yes, you should," Tabitha agreed, noticing that Lady Lydford was trembling, for which she could not blame her. "I wonder who he was. . . ."

"I did not see his face," Lord Ashton said. "If I had, he would have heard from my seconds, by God! Did you recognize him, Kate?"

She nodded her head and looked at him anxiously. "It was Lord Marlton," she said a bit too casually as she exchanged a secret glance with her brother, who returned the look and nodded so slightly as to go unnoticed by Tabitha. "I beg you not to be so fierce, Lion."

"Lions are fierce," he said grimly, "when those they love are in danger."

"Well, my dear, the danger's past," Lady Lydford said, but there was still a little tremor in her voice.

Once they were back at the stables and dismounted, Lord Ashton said to Tabitha, "I am afraid that I have not yet asked after Lady Laura. How is she feeling?"

"She is better. She had a cold but is better enough to come downstairs in the afternoon."

"I am sorry to hear she has been ill. Perhaps I might call on her later today? I am sure Katherine would like to meet her."

"And I am certain Laura would be delighted," Tabitha assured him. "She has been wanting to thank you for bringing her home after the accident."

"Shall we say three?"

"That would be a very good hour. I will tell her to expect you." Tabitha smiled.

"Three o'clock! He is coming to see me at three o'clock?" Laura said delightedly. "Oh, dear," she sighed a second later. "I must look so very pale."

70

"On the contrary," Tabitha responded. "I have seldom seen you looking so blooming. Is that not true, Aunt Ellen?"

"Entirely, my love," Miss Parry agreed rather dryly. "You are not of an age, my dear Laura, when a cold will leave you with a pale and wasted countenance."

"In fact," Tabitha added unkindly, and untruthfully, "your nose seems rather red."

"Oh, let me have a mirror!" Laura cried. She peered in the looking glass. "It does not. What a tabby cat you are! To make amends, let your abigail come to me, Tabitha, for I want to look my best, and silly Betsy dresses my hair in such a girlish way, no matter what I say. I will wear my rose-colored peignoir or should I dress? No, I think not, else he will not think me ill at all. I do not want him to believe his visit all in vain."

"I am sure that would never occur to him," Tabitha said soothingly, "but you cannot receive a gentleman, undressed and in your bedchamber."

"No, not at all," said Miss Parry. "If he were a close relative, and you were convalescing after a long and dangerous illness, or if you were on your deathbed and bidding farewell to your friends . . ."

"But I expect that Lord Ashton will retain his garment," Laura said pertly.

"If you are feeling so unwell that you wish to change into your nightclothes, Laura, you are still too ill to leave your chamber and receive a caller," said Miss Parry, "and that is my last word on the subject." She hurried from the room.

Tabitha expected a *pro forma* appeal from her sister, but Laura said nothing. Good heavens, was her little sister finally growing up?

"IT IS MOST KIND of Lord Ashton to bring his sister to call on Laura," Miss Parry commented as she and Tabitha waited together in the withdrawing room. "Lady Lydford's visit will certainly cheer her. She has been so very fretful, having to stay indoors these past long days."

"I noticed that," Tabitha said dryly. "What a pity she's so prone to colds." She thought it much more likely that the prospect of being able to receive gentlemen again would improve Laura's temperament than a visit from a kindly lady some twenty years her senior.

"I," Miss Parry said tartly, "have been rather pleased by her indisposition. At least it has kept her out of mischief for the nonce." She had an acerbic look for Tabitha. "I wish that I could say the same for you! It is a wonder Lord Ashton has been so attentive. Still, he might wish to keep on good terms with the family. I find it exceedingly promising that he is coming to see your sister."

"You are not suggesting that he has become interested in Laura, are you?" Tabitha asked, hoping that she did not sound too much like the dog in the manger.

"My dear, I am not saying that he is deeply interested in her—he might prefer you . . . but do let us be honest with each other. He will need to marry again. He is the last male of his line, and naturally, he will want a young woman from a family equal with his own.

"And someone who can provide him with sons. I know you have a *tendre* for him, but you are past your first youth and Laura is only eighteen. And my dear, considering his own sad experience, we can be sure that he is aware of the dangers of childbearing for an older woman."

Tabitha felt a heavy pounding in her throat. "But, he asked me, not Laura, to ride with him and his sister," she reminded her aunt.

"He could not ask Laura, not when she has a cold. Did you notice that by planning to arrive at three he has arranged to be among the earliest callers? He may even have a few moments here alone."

"Lady Lydford will be with him, and I hardly think that you and I will absent ourselves. And since he does know why she was so confined, I don't imagine he's much interested in a hoyden," Tabitha replied, thinking, I can not bear it if he loves Laura. If it were anyone else I would never have to see him after this Season, but if he marries Laura, I'll not be able to avoid him all the time.

"Alas, yes, but she is young, and gentlemen have a way of forgiving pretty, young girls. And racing in the park is not a terrible social sin. I find it a very good sign that he wishes to see her, in spite of the contretemps in the park. I am sure he likes you, my dear, but men in his position, as you well know, need heirs. I do not say this to hurt you, Tabitha, but merely to remind you that you must not build your hopes on something that has no real foundation."

Tabitha sometimes wondered if, nine years ago, her aunt had done her best to keep her away from Lord Ashton. Miss Parry had not even allowed him to pay his respects to the mourning household, and she had come swiftly out of church and interrupted their last conversation very summarily.

Why? Tabitha wondered. But it was too late for the speculations that had troubled her on the way home to Derbyshire, which had been forgotten in the necessity for comforting her bereaved family. Now she found herself wondering again. Had her aunt really been eager to quash her poor little romantic dreams? And now was she determined to further Laura's chances with the same man?

Tabitha firmly reminded herself that her inconsistent aunt often did things for no reason apparent to anyone else. Sometimes she started a project, only to abandon it without ever offering a word of explanation. Tabitha doubted that she always had a reason.

"In case you are wondering why I hope that Lord Ashton has an interest in Laura," Miss Parry said with a startling perspicacity, "it's because the sooner your sister is creditably settled, the better. It will be better for all three of us. Her escapade in the park is, to my mind, a harbinger of mad starts to come if she is not quickly given some real responsibility. To my thinking, her spirits are far too high and her self-control too weak. She could easily commit a solecism that disgraces both herself and the family."

"Oh, come, Aunt Ellen," Tabitha said coolly, "surely you are exaggerating. True, Laura is high-spirited. . . ."

"And devious and nearly unmanageable. She needs an older husband, one who has had the experience of marriage, one who is firm, yet tactful. To my thinking, Lord Ashton is the man who could handle her very effectively. I am sure she will be a much happier girl once she is married."

Miss Parry paused for a moment, then added, "And while I do not wish to distress you, for I know it is a topic you tend to avoid, the circumstance of your father's death may discourage some less . . . forgiving member of the ton."

"Most of those same gentlemen keep mistresses of their own," Tabitha observed. "Who are they to judge?"

"There are certain aspects of life, Tabitha, which are a gentleman's province, and with which a lady should not be connected in any way. It is known that you, Laura's sister, were at the theater that night. . . ."

Her aunt was riding roughshod over her feelings, and Tabitha was tempted to mention that she, Laura's aunt, had also been present the night Lord Sterling, her brother-in-law, was murdered, but she refrained.

There was considerable sense in what her aunt was

saying. Plenty of flighty young girls became more staid matrons, and her father's death had been a scandal, Tabitha reasoned dolefully. And she, herself, felt too old to consider marriage. But all this did not mean that Lord Ashton was interested in Laura.

"It does seem," she began, "rather a lot to ask of a man, to be given an unformed girl from which to produce a suitable wife, while most men expect their bride's family to have performed that task for them."

The bells of London began to strike the hour of three, answering each other's chimes across the city. Laura ran into the room. "That silly little clock in my room is five minutes slow. Thank heavens *he* has not arrived."

She ran to the sofa and lay upon it and arranged her skirts prettily about her. "Oh," she cried, and stood up.

"I am glad to see you have realized the impropriety of lounging," said Miss Parry.

"It isn't that. I just remembered that my best profile is from the right." She prepared to lie down again, so as to show off that side of her face.

"I wasn't aware that you had more than two profiles, dear. You had better sit here, in the armchair. Lord Ashton won't be pleased if you are lying down. Gentlemen don't like sickly females, and you might distress Lady Lydford if she thinks you are still to weak to be up and about."

"Do tell me what she is like," Laura said, taking her seat in the chair. "I understand that she hasn't any sisters. I wonder if she is lonely."

"I thought she was a very pleasant lady," Tabitha replied. "Why do you want to know if she has sisters?"

"I merely wondered," said Laura, airily.

Tabitha had a sudden suspicion that Laura wondered if Lady Lydford had any interest in acquiring by marriage the sister which nature had denied her.

"Lady Lydford and Lord Ashton," announced the butler, showing in the visitors.

"How nice to see you again, Lord Ashton," said Miss Parry. She was behaving as if the unfortunate scene in the library had never taken place. Tabitha wondered if she ought to have warned Laura not to mention it, but surely even Laura, even if she had not been particularly contrite, had not missed Miss Parry's displeasure over the incident.

Introductions were performed, and then Lord Ashton walked over to Laura. "Little Lady Laura, you are looking much more the thing."

She smiled up at him. "Oh, I am quite recovered, my lord. In fact, I am hardly ever ill. Tabitha will confirm it. I am most hardy."

"I am delighted to hear that." He turned to Tabitha. "I see that the Spencers are sturdy stock."

"Oh very," interjected Laura. "Mama had seven children, and all save Alice are living. And Imogen has two children, and James three, and William four, and most of them are boys." That was true: there were five boys and four girls.

"Quite a mathematical progression," said Lord Ashton, smiling.

"And they are all blessed with excellent health," said Miss Parry, making it firmly understood that constitution, not reproductive prowess, was being discussed.

Lord Ashton went to sit by Tabitha on the sofa. As she watched him, the quotation, "The glass of fashion and the mold of form" came to mind. Why did the dashed man have to be so handsome? But could she honestly say she would not care for him had he been plain?

"Henry has gone to Tattersall, Lord Ashton," said Laura. "I hope you did not expect to see him."

"I called chiefly so my sister could meet the ladies of the house," came his reply.

"Have you any news of Lord Lydford?" asked Tabitha, addressing Lady Lydford. It was not a very original opening to a conversation, but it was better than listening to Laura fishing for compliments.

"I had a letter some days ago. Despite my fears for him, Lion is right. My husband writes of nothing more alarming than attacks of mosquitoes. And he sent me a pretty picture of an Indian woman and her papoose—that is the word for native babies—drawn by an old French trapper."

"Oh, I love babies," said Laura. "I do wish I could have one of my very own."

"In time, Lady Laura," said Lady Lydford. "Now you should be enjoying the freedom of youth."

"I do not find it so very free," she grumbled. "All those silly strictures. I am never allowed to do any of the things that I want to."

No, thought Tabitha, but permitted or not, you do them anyway. I wonder what would happen if we removed all restrictions. Without the thrill of misbehaving, would any of your exploits have the same allure?

"They are there for your protection, my dear," said Miss Parry, "and I do not imagine that you really wish to do anything foolish or unwise."

"But it is so unfair," protested Laura. "By the time I am old enough to do anything, I'll be too old to have fun."

Tabitha was amused to hear Laura voice the same opinion she had recalled a few days earlier.

"I think you will not find that to be the case as you grow older," said Lady Lydford. From her tone it was clear that she, too, was amused.

"I cannot imagine life after twenty," Laura said with a little shudder. "For a gentleman, it might be interesting, but for a lady?"

"I am sure that Lady Tabitha, Miss Parry, and my sister would not agree with you there. Each stage of life brings its own joys," said Lord Ashton.

"But after a while, one is too old for love," Laura said petulantly.

"Now that is patently untrue," said Lady Lydford. "If I might offer my own case: when I was nineteen, the young man I had pledged myself to died of smallpox. For many years I felt that I could never love another, and then that I would never meet his equal. I was thirty when I accepted my husband's proposal, and I can tell you, Lady Laura, that we are not unique in being a happy and loving couple."

"Do you have children?" Miss Parry asked anxiously.

"A little girl and a trio of ruffians," she answered.

"Heaven be praised."

Tabitha suddenly recalled a book of engravings of Quebec City in the library, and asked Lady Lydford if she had seen it. When that lady expressed interest in looking at anything having to do with the country where her husband was staying, Laura was dispatched to fetch it.

Miss Parry and Lady Lydford fell into conversation about childhood illnesses. Under cover of their chatter, Lord Ashton quietly asked Tabitha if she was fully recovered from her misadventure.

"Yes, thank you." It was not perfectly true. The cuts had not completely healed, but she knew she was on the mend. "And thank you for coming to my rescue, and for the lovely roses. I did not like to mention it when I saw you this morning, in front of Lady Lydford, in case she had not heard of my foolish encounter."

"I have not told anyone, but I expect it will be a nine-days' wonder about town. There were too many people at the British Museum for word not to have gotten out. But please, do not worry about it. It will soon blow over."

"I had thought to write to you, but it is not the sort of letter our governesses taught us to compose in the schoolroom. I fear that is a very poor excuse, my lord."

"It is original, but it is a fault that does not need excuse, if it can be called a fault. I am not aware of any convention demanding that one writes letters thanking men for throwing people down staircases."

"But one ought to try."

"Perhaps you could write a copy book of letters for people to use in unusual circumstances." Jestingly, Lord Ashton suggested a couple of humorous examples.

Laura returned with the book, and proceeded to arrange the party to her liking. She put Lord Ashton on her left and Lady Lydford on the right, and turned the pages with a running commentary on the engravings. The captions, however, were in French, and soon Lord Ashton had vacated his place so that Tabitha, who was proficient where Laura was not, could translate them.

He stood behind her, resting his arm on the back of the sofa. Tabitha was acutely aware of his hand, inches from her neck. After a few more minutes other visitors were announced, and a little while later Lady Lydford and Lord Ashton took their leave.

After a long afternoon of entertaining callers, Miss Parry went upstairs to rest before dinner. Laura came to sit next to Tabitha and began to sing Lord Ashton's praises.

"Is he the only man you notice?" asked Tabitha. "It is foolish to become particularly attached to one gentleman so early in the Season."

"Oh, he is not the only one—certainly not the only one who notices me—but he is the best catch."

"You are a mercenary little thing," said Tabitha crossly. "Don't you want a husband who holds you in esteem, a husband you care for?"

"But they all like me," Laura said. "So I might as well choose the best. And, I adore Lord Ashton."

"Well, for heaven's sake, don't say that in public. It doesn't do for a lady to wear her heart on her sleeve," Tabitha warned.

"Really, do you think I have no manners? I'm going upstairs to dress." Laura flounced out of the room, then stuck her head around the door to add, "You should be careful where you wear yours," before running off.

Did her sister realize that her own feelings for Lord Ashton had reawakened? Tabitha doubted it. Who could have told Laura what her sister had once felt when she had confided in no one? It was just another example of Laura's rudenesses.

It was time that Tabitha came to a decision about her love for Lord Ashton. Her attempts to ruthlessly kill it, as she thought she had done years before, were not successful.

So she would try a different approach. She would allow herself to enjoy his company, to reflect upon him as much as possible. There was nothing she could do to try to fix his interest. She was not the sort of woman to throw her cap over the windmill—even as she thought it there came a perverse pleasure that she had not yet taken to wearing caps—and, truth be told, Lord Ashton obviously had no interest to fix.

And either the flame would burn out, or it would not. In either case, she would be no worse off than she was now. After the Season she would return home to Derbyshire and start wearing caps.

But the thought of life in the midst of her family, yet alone, was too much to bear. Fine, she would not suppress her feelings toward Lord Ashton, but she also would not close her mind to the possibility of finding another man to be her husband. Very likely, once she met this hypothetical gentleman, her foolish, schoolgirl feeling for Lord Ashton would vanish. And at that point, if not right now, she would say good riddance.

== 8 ==

"I vow," Miss Parry said as she came slowly down the stairs to join Tabitha and Laura in the drawing room. "My head whirls. It seems that no sooner are we bid to one rout, three other hostesses demand our, or rather, your presence, my dears."

She regarded her nieces warmly. "You have both had a most remarkable success. But I cannot understand why neither of you is tired! I would like nothing more than a week of rest!"

"I, too," Tabitha agreed. "But I am sure that Laura is not of that persuasion."

"No." Laura laughed. "I cannot say that I am. It has been monstrous pleasant to be always in demand. And to meet so many interesting people." She sighed, adding wistfully, "But I do wish I could have met Lord Byron."

"Byron!" Miss Parry shuddered. "I thank God that you did not! I am also thankful that he has left England. When I think of his poor wife. . . ."

"I am sorry for his marital difficulties, but he is a wonderful poet," Tabitha said.

"I believe we should be going," Miss Parry said impatiently. "And remember, I do not wish to remain overlong. One must always be standing at a rout, and my back aches after an hour or so. And I find the chatter too hard on my ears."

She paused, adding in less fretful tones, "I must say that both of you are looking your best. That particular shade of blue is precisely the color of your eyes, Tabitha, and yellow has always been a flattering shade for you, Laura."

"Thank you, Aunt Ellen." Laura smiled. "One must be very grateful to Henry for recommending that mantua-maker. I do wish he would come home. He could take us to Vauxhall Gardens. Cornelia says that it is delightful."

"It is not an appropriate place for a young girl," Miss Parry replied. "There are all manner of undesirable types lurking in the gardens. I wonder that your friend Cornelia has been allowed to visit them."

"She was with her mother. They both found it much to their taste," Laura said pettishly.

"Do let us be going if we are going," Tabitha said. She was feeling tired and out of sorts. Since Lord Ashton's visit over two weeks ago, she had not seen him. Her resolution to enjoy his company remained untested, but she found that when she did not try to prevent them, memories of him disturbed her less.

She hoped he would be present today, since Lady Stuart's routs were generally very well-attended. She wondered if he had gone out of town. His principal estate was located in Warwickshire.

She sighed. It did no good to try to guess where he might be. If only her infatuation would burn itself out. She wished she could prevent herself from missing him as much as she did, and that she was not looking for his face at every rout, dance, or picnic. She wanted to see him.

Tabitha stifled another sigh as Miss Parry, acting on her exhortation, moved toward the hall. Routs, Tabitha thought, were all the same: a great deal of talk, gossip, and new people, though this, of course, was important for Laura. Her sister was very hard to please. She had met several eligible young men and had received enough bouquets to fill a hothouse, but none of their senders appeared to interest her.

Tabitha hoped that today would be different. In common with Aunt Ellen, she sincerely hoped that Laura would be spoken for in the very near future, though she and her aunt were agreed that they would not force a match on her. Indeed, it was doubtful that she could be forced. She was very stubborn, and she had a penchant for handsome men.

She had already stated that she would turn down offers, if they were made from several eligible gentlemen who did not meet her standards of masculine beauty. But she had always sworn to end the Season an engaged woman.

"Tabitha." Miss Parry broke into her thoughts. "I begin to believe you hard of hearing. That is the second time I have called you. We are leaving."

"Yes, Aunt Ellen." Tabitha sighed, wishing she need not go, wishing it were near the end of the day, and wondering once more why Lord Ashton had not called of late.

Lady Stuart dwelt in a large, handsome house on Charles Street. Though it much resembled other houses on that street, its entrance hall was a definite departure from custom. Lady Stuart was a fanatical Scot and her hall was adorned with near–life-size murals depicting Mary of Scotland accepting the crown, St. Columba preaching in Scotland, and the defeat of Edward II at the Battle of Bannockburn. Lady Stuart even claimed that her husband, Sir Angus, was distant kin to Mary of Scotland. This fervor for things Scottish was the butt of much witticism among the ton. It was said to be even affecting the Prince Regent. Certainly he was known to be a great admirer of Lady Stuart.

Lady Stuart bore little trace of her own Scottish ancestry. She was a short, plump woman of some forty years of age who, as Laura whispered, should not have worn the diaphanous green gown, which only emphasized her girth. Her hair was of a shade of red which suggested the dye bottle rather than an inherited hue, and unfortunately clashed with the tartan scarf she wore.

Tabitha, after a quelling glance at Laura, quickly put her hand out to greet her hostess who, peering at her shortsightedly, said, "You must be dear Lady Laura."

"No, I am Tabitha," she said quickly.

"Oh." Lady Stuart turned to Laura. "Fancy, I thought you were older and she younger. Your sister has a lovely skin, my dear."

Tabitha bit down a laugh. She had a strong feeling that from Laura's sulky look, her sister had not appreciated their hostess's confusion.

They were shepherded into a hall and up a flight of stairs into a vast chamber which was filled with people whose faces and names Tabitha was beginning to recognize easily, since she encountered them again and again. However, there still were numerous faces she did not recognize as her hostess made the introductions. Finally, Lady Stuart seemed to feel that she had done her duty as hostess and left Tabitha and her aunt to their own devices.

Laura had already sighted some new friends across the room and had quickly made her way toward them. Unbecoming behavior which Tabitha noted unhappily. The fact that it brought her considerable masculine admiration did nothing to assuage Tabitha's chagrin at Laura's very coming ways. What did her sister want, she wondered, or rather, whom did she want?

For a moment Tabitha thought she saw Sir Frederick, but when she peered in that direction, she saw only a man of similar height. Recalling what Lord Ashton had told her of the baronet, she doubted Lady Stuart had invited him.

Tabitha's thoughts were interrupted as a certain Lady Desmond, whom Miss Parry had met at another rout, came up to them to pour into their ears the latest *on-dit* concerning the Prince Regent. Lady Desmond's gossip drifted to events and people unknown to Tabitha, who ceased to pay much attention.

"Tabitha, my dear," her aunt said, "I fear you are woolgathering."

"No, I would never credit that," a man's voice said. "She looks as if she were caught in some wonderful dream. I would like to see her painted in just such a pose."

Guiltily returning from her thoughts, Tabitha found her hostess attempting to present a gentleman of medium height, fashionably dressed, and not ill-looking despite a thin scar that ran down the side of his face from brow to chin, suggesting a sword wound. She wondered if it had been sustained in battle. He had brown hair and eyes of so light a hazel that they almost seemed yellow. She had an instant recollection of having seen such a gaze recently, but when and where it was, she had no notion.

As these thoughts swept through her mind, Lady Stuart said, "My dear Lady Tabitha, I would like to present Lord Marlton, an old friend of mine. And this, my dear Felix, is Lady Tabitha Spencer."

"Ah." Lord Marlton bowed over her hand. "I am delighted to make your acquaintance, my lady."

"And I am pleased to meet you, my lord," Tabitha murmured politely, even though she was not quite sure she meant it. Then it occurred to her—this was the man who had so frightened Lady Lydford when they rode in the park. And there was something else about him—a tantalizing recollection which she could not place.

As these thoughts sped through her mind, she exchanged polite pleasantries. After a few moments, he fixed his eyes on Tabitha again and said, "It is so uncommonly noisy in here, one can scarcely think, let alone engage a lady in conversation. May I have the pleasure of calling on you, Lady Tabitha?"

Tabitha suddenly found herself wanting to give him a flat refusal, but since she had no reason to do so, she said politely, "I should be delighted, my lord."

"May I hope that you will receive me tomorrow?" he asked.

She could almost hear her aunt's acquiescent thought, and she did feel a small touch at her elbow. "Of course," she said with a slight smile.

His own smile was triumphant. "Tomorrow, then," he repeated, adding regretfully, "I must leave now . . . but I will see you tomorrow."

"Yes, my lord, tomorrow," Tabitha murmured, wondering again why he made her so uneasy.

"Well, my dear," Miss Parry said as Lord Marlton left them, "I think you have made quite a conquest, and such a charming man, do you not agree? So unlike his cousin."

Before Tabitha could respond, Miss Parry added, "Indeed, I think it was a case of love at first sight!"

"And I am of the opinion that you are refining upon it far too much," Tabitha said coolly, hoping against hope that her aunt was wrong and then wondering why she did not like Lord Marlton. Usually, she did not reach conclusions so hastily. Keeping that in mind, perhaps it was as well she was seeing him again, because to be fair, she might be wrong. She rather hoped she was not.

And the rest of the evening was a flat disappointment. Lord Ashton did not appear. Tabitha meant to ask her aunt who Lord Marlton's cousin was, but as they drove home, Laura's chatter dominated the conversation, and by the next day she had forgotten about it.

Lord Marlton lived on Curzon Street in a large square house. Seen from the front, it had a pillared portico flanked by a pair of windows. It rose three stories, each with a paucity of windows which gave it a closed, even secretive look—at least so it appeared to Tabitha. Indeed, it seemed to loom over her, especially on this day when its sun-thrown shadow engulfed the carriageway leading to its entrance. She did not share these thoughts with Miss Parry, for she was honest enough to admit that her lack of enthusiasm for its owner might have blighted her vision.

She did not precisely dislike him. During his visit to her house, his behavior had been quite unexceptional. However, rather than being flattered by what her aunt called his obviously deep regard for her, she could only wish he had disliked her on sight.

Miss Parry's stubborn insistence that she would find him more to her taste as their acquaintance deepened depressed her, for she was positive that she would not like him better, no matter how well she knew him. That Miss Parry already regarded him as her suitor not only depressed but also frightened her a little, too.

The idea of being pursued by Lord Marlton was deeply repugnant to Tabitha. Of course, she had to admit that the only so-called pursuit that she would ever favor was that of Lord Ashton, still inexplicably absent. He was not out of town, for Henry, returning to London after a week visiting his wife, had mentioned seeing Lord Ashton at White's that very afternoon. He had further informed them that Ashton had won a large sum playing piquet.

"He has the devil's own luck," Henry had said enviously.

That comment had been particularly painful to Tabitha since in addition to abolishing her hope that he was out of town, it set her to wondering where he was. No doubt other houses knew him, houses where dwelt marriageable daughters, or possibly merry widows.

"Tabitha," Miss Parry said sharply. "We have arrived."

Tabitha tensed. "I am sorry," she replied. "I was thinking."

"Obviously, but the footman is waiting to hand you down."

"I am sorry," Tabitha said again, seeing the coach door was open. She descended, wishing that they were a hundred miles distant and heartily envying Laura, who had been left at the house of Lady Pamela Preston, one of her new friends. Laura had been included in the invitation to view Lord Marlton's paintings, but she had refused to go, saying that she did not like him.

Miss Parry had been quite annoyed by the comment, saying that he was quite exceptional. Now, stepping reluctantly out of the carriage, Tabitha was conscious of a strong desire to return to that vehicle and order the coachman to drive her home. Dismissing such an impossible thought, she dutifully mounted the steps to the front door.

In her mind were the confidences given her aunt by Lady Stuart and repeated to herself by Miss Parry.

"She told me that he fought under Wellington in the Peninsula and was twice wounded—hence his scar and limp. Shortly after he arrived home from Spain, his wife died of an inflammation of the lungs.

"Lady Stuart tells me that he married Lady Marlton, who was Phoebe Lassiter, you know, as an act of kindness. Her father did him a great disservice once, but he forgave him when he was dying, and married his daughter and made her a lady. She left a child, a son, but Lord Marlton seems indifferent. He is very lonely," Miss Parry had concluded, "and he has vainly tried to solace himself with collecting paintings and traveling."

He had certainly had a sad life, Tabitha thought, and he was to be pitied. Her musing came to an end as they reached the door and Miss Parry let the knocker fall against its plate.

It was opened almost immediately by a thin, grave-looking butler, who, being informed of their identities, appeared graver than ever as he admitted them.

They stepped into a lofty entrance hall with a wide expanse of polished floor and a dark blue ceiling set with white intaglios and centered by a magnificent crystal chandelier. The door leading to the other apartments was painted white, and above it was a half-arc adorned with a bas-relief depicting nymphs at play.

Before Tabitha had a chance to absorb any more details, Lord Marlton appeared, clad as usual in his understated but elegant garb. With him was a thin lady he introduced as Miss Blodworth—his elderly cousin who had come to be their hostess. He greeted both ladies with enthusiasm, but even while he was speaking to Miss Parry, his eyes had strayed to Tabitha's face, something of which she was all too aware.

She was also aware of his deep, almost greedy admiration for her, and, as usual, it made her feel exceedingly uncomfortable. Indeed, she had a strong desire to plead a headache and leave immediately. As this was clearly impossible, she must attend to what her host was saying.

"Dear Lady Tabitha, I have waited for this day," he said. "Please come in here." He indicated a door across the hall, and positioning himself between his two guests, he led them to a large withdrawing room, the walls of which were hung with superb oil paintings. Miss Blodworth, who had said nothing beyond "How do you do," followed.

This room was also beautifully furnished, but it was the way the paintings were arranged that caught Tabitha's eyes. On both sides of the chamber were large landscapes set between pairs of smaller portraits above and below them.

However, she only glimpsed them, for her host led his guests through that room and across a hall to a room which, she guessed, must run the whole width of the house. Here, she was dazzled by the paintings thronging the walls.

At her aunt's inquiries, names Tabitha knew and those she did not tripped from Lord Marlton's tongue: Holbein, Breugel, Raphael, Botticelli, Titian, Rembrandt. She felt overwhelmed by the beauty of the paintings, to the point that she was relieved when he asked them to take tea and led them into a small withdrawing room.

Miss Blodworth rang a small crystal bell, and a stalwart footman bore in a massive silver tray on which there was an elegant tea service of Mr. Wedgwood's small fragile china cups. Lord Marlton served the tea himself, explaining that it was a special blend made especially for him in China.

Tabitha and Miss Blodworth sat in silence while Miss Parry praised the paintings.

Lord Marlton pronounced himself gratified by her good judgment. "However," he said, "they are not all here. The best of them," he looked at Tabitha, "are in my house in Somerset. Those are the works I esteem above all others."

"They must be beautiful, indeed," Miss Parry said.

"Yes, I must agree. They are unique, I believe." He fell into a brief silence. Then he said, "But I fear you will think me far too proud. I do not mean to be, but I have a passion for all things beautiful." His eyes were on Tabitha's face as he repeated, "Yes, a passion. In certain ways, I have been able to gratify that passion, though, alas, not in all ways. I hope I do not sound too greedy."

"Oh, no, not in the least," Miss Parry assured him. "I imagine that all of us, no matter how blessed by the world's goods we may be, long for that which we have not yet attained."

"How very understanding you are, my dear Miss Parry," he said warmly.

He had addressed her aunt, but his gaze had never left Tabitha's face, and she had the uncomfortable feeling that his words were also addressed to her.

His meaning was, unfortunately, all too clear, and she wished strongly that she had the courage to give him the set-down he deserved. One that would acquaint him with the fact that she was not to be hung on a wall or set on a table or, she thought with a little shudder, locked in a cabinet. If he chose to increase his collection, she wished he would look elsewhere.

=== 9 ===

WHEN FINALLY THEY LEFT and were in their carriage returning home, Miss Parry broke a brief silence by saying in tones close to ecstasy, "Lord Marlton is very deeply in love with you, my dear, but I am sure you are quite aware of that."

"I presume," Tabitha said carefully, "that he might have a certain regard for me, but I cannot say that it is returned, Aunt Ellen."

Miss Parry raised her eyebrows. "I do not understand you," she said in surprise. "He is wealthy, well-born, and if he is not precisely handsome, he has fine features, and furthermore he is the scion of a very old family. Lady Stuart told me that one of his ancestors fought at Agincourt."

"He is hardly the only man in London who can claim that heritage," Tabitha said coolly. "Furthermore, Aunt Ellen, even allowing all you have said about him to be true, there is something about him I cannot like."

"And what, pray, might that be?" Miss Parry demanded acerbically.

Tabitha hesitated. "I do not know . . . I only know that he does not please me. That is all I can tell you."

"Oh, indeed, well, there is a great deal more that I can tell you," Miss Parry said crossly. "You have not been showered with offers, my dear. Granted we've not been in London long, but even without the gift of prescience, I would predict that you are not likely to receive many more, given the fact that you are in your later twenties."

There was a moment's silence. Tabitha wondered what answer she could give that would close the subject.

Then her aunt spoke again. "I might tell you, also, that I was of your mind when I was, say . . . twenty-five. Someone offered for me and I did not accept even though I, like you, was beyond the age when one can expect to receive offers. I was sure that there would be other men who would ask for my hand. There was one man in particular—I expect I was waiting for him—but he married another and I remained as you see—useful to my family as you are useful now. You are considerably more attractive than I ever was, but they want young females, my dear, young females who will give them young families."

"I am not beyond the age of childbearing, Aunt Ellen," Tabitha said sharply.

"And," Miss Parry said sagely, "you are still attracted to Lord Ashton, and it is possible that he is aware of it—which is why he has ceased to call."

The carriage drew to a stop; to Tabitha's relief they had arrived home. Upon entering the house, she hurried immediately upstairs to her bedchamber, but her aunt determinedly followed her, waiting only until Tabitha had divested herself of her cloak.

"As I was saying—" Miss Parry began.

"I remember what you were saying," Tabitha interrupted. "And I say that women have been known to bear children even after the advanced age of forty!"

"It does not happen often, my love. And often a woman who has her first child when she's thirty or more has grave difficulties. There is a history in our family. My poor sister, and your sister Alice. And look at Lord Ashton's first wife."

"And his sister. Lady Lydford was thirty when she married. She must have been older than that when her first child was born."

"I do not think that three out of four makes very good odds. Fie, that I should speak so irreverently of such sorrow."

"I am only twenty-seven," protested Tabitha.

"And often a couple are married a good year or more before their first child comes. I would think twice before I refused Lord Marlton's offer."

"He has not yet offered," Tabitha reminded her.

"He will, and soon," Miss Parry said. "Perhaps the next time he comes here. And you know what I think you should do."

"I will not, Aunt Ellen, not even at the risk of remaining single forever!"

"And will you tend Imogen at her next lying-in, and when Henry's wife has another child, will you let yourself be summoned? And when Laura marries . . ."

Tabitha regarded her coolly. "Please, Aunt Ellen, I pray you will not continue in this vein."

Moving to her side, Miss Parry clutched Tabitha's arm. "I wish only to remind you what lies in store for a single female from a large family. You are so beautiful, Tabitha. You have kept your looks much, much longer than is usual . . . but in three years, you will be thirty and in five more, you will be thirty-five.

"Your brothers and sisters will be saying, 'Let's fetch Aunt Tabitha . . . she can see to the Presentation . . . she can take care of dearest Imogen after her difficult confinement . . . she can oversee James's wedding . . . she can tend his bride when she is with child.'

"Oh, Aunt Ellen." Tabitha hurried to her side. "I am sorry . . . I never thought . . . I mean, you have never let me know. I suppose I should have realized how difficult it is for you . . . all these duties, year after year." She put her arms around her aunt, repeating, "I am so very, very sorry."

Miss Parry leaned against her for a moment. "Tabitha, my dear, you are quite the most beautiful of my nieces and also the kindest. And I am afraid that once I did you a grave disservice."

"You?" Tabitha questioned. "I cannot believe it." There were times when her aunt nearly drove her to distraction, but she could not imagine anything Aunt Ellen had done or said that could be described as a grave disservice.

Her aunt moved away from her. "You may not believe it, my dear. It is true. It was when Lord Lovell, as he was then, was first beginning to court you. I am now deeply, deeply sorry for my actions at that time. It was not, however, all my fault. I mean, keeping you apart . . . not letting him pay his respects after your father's death . . . not letting him speak overlong to you at the funeral."

She sat down. "There were the conventions, but I could have been more lenient in my interpretation of the rules, more understanding. I hope you will forgive me."

Tabitha said gently, "It was more convention than it was you, Aunt Ellen. Furthermore, we had reached no understanding, and even if we had my year of mourning must have precluded it."

"I am not sure of that. He wrote to me, asking permission to write to you, and I said no. You see, there was so much to be done. My poor sister was already ill, and little James and Laura beside themselves. All the arrangements for putting off William's wedding—I know Mildred's family was responsible, but William blithely promised my services, and I was up until midnight writing letters on your mother's behalf, and about the wretched wedding.

"And then, the very day the letter came, Imogen developed that putrid fever, and we were in fear of her life. I just couldn't cope without you. I just couldn't face the idea of your getting married and going away, and leaving it all to me."

"But even if he had written, I could have hardly become engaged very quickly, and I certainly wouldn't have married the year Papa died, even if William waited only six months."

"I know that now, my dear, but at the time I was too overcome to think clearly. I dispatched a couple of lines while I was sitting up with Imogen. . . . Oh, my dear, I am so very sorry."

"It is nothing to worry about, dear Aunt. I am sure that if he wanted to write to me so very badly, he would have appealed later. And you would have relented."

"Of course. But I am not sure I did not stand in the way of your happiness."

"I am certain you did not," Tabitha said, willing herself to believe it. "But I beg you, do not try to force me into the arms of Lord Marlton."

"I wish . . ." Miss Parry sighed. "But no, I will not try to further this match if you hold him in such dislike. Yet you are so beautiful, Tabitha, and so kind. I cannot bear to think of you living on the outside of life as I have done."

"I do not feel that I am living on the outside, Aunt Ellen," Tabitha assured her gently. "Now . . . if you will excuse me, I think I must rest."

"Let me ask you just one more thing, my dear."

"Very well." Tabitha did not see how she could banish her aunt from her bedchamber without making that lady feel that she had incurred her niece's displeasure.

"You do not dislike Lord Marlton because of his cousin, do you?"

Tabitha recalled the remark her aunt had made at Lady Stuart's rout. "I am afraid that I don't know anything about his cousin."

"It is somewhat painful, my dear. I know you never like to speak of your father's death. I rather think you are ignorant of some of the details."

Tabitha had never wished to know the details. Her father was dead, and if, as the years went by, she learned that he had not been the paragon she had imagined, she accepted the fact that he was only human. Whatever sort of husband and friend he had been, nothing altered the fact that he had loved her, and that she missed him.

Other members of the family had read the printed reports, anxious for any news of the event, but Tabitha had wanted to know as little about it as possible. Her habit of not reading the newspapers and journals came from that time, for she knew that even now some wits made reference to Lord Sterling's untimely and undignified death.

"You know he was shot, of course," Miss Parry was saying. "You were there. And I imagine you know that young man shot him because he was a rival for the affections of a girl from the opera ballet."

"I gathered that."

"Well, the young man was Lord Marlton's cousin. Apparently he loved this girl to distraction, but she found him . . . unnatural and cruel. When her lover pressed her to marry him, she refused, giving her affair with your father as the reason. The young man felt that she was sullied, and no longer wanted her. He took his revenge on your father and did away with himself, knowing full well that he would cause a scandal."

"Why didn't he kill the girl?" Tabitha asked. "Or did he, and I just never heard of it?"

"Who can understand the workings of a madman's mind? I understand he left a long letter, claiming that he could not live without her, but wanted her to remain alive, suffering, as he had while he lived."

"What an unpleasant story," Tabitha said. "I am amazed that Lord Marlton wants anything to do with the Spencers."

"He is a very forgiving man," her aunt said. "And I dare say the matter need never be mentioned between you."

Tabitha tried to imagine a marriage so constrained that the husband could never refer to the fact that his wife's father had been killed by his own cousin. She found it as difficult to imagine one where the topic was openly aired.

She took a moment to collect her thoughts, composed a speech, and spoke. "Dear Aunt Ellen, I know you are trying to make amends for something you perceive as a fault, but I bear you no ill will, and I very much doubt that your actions had any influence on Lord Ashton. I am not averse to marriage, but I will not marry where I feel no affection, and Lord Marlton does not inspire any warm emotion in me. I promise, however, that I will listen most carefully to, and consider most thoroughly, the address of any other gentleman."

"But you refused an offer just before you came away," protested Miss Parry.

"I did not say I would accept any offer, but I also say that I will not reject a suitor out-of-hand. And Aunt Ellen, I wrote to William directly upon our arrival, asking that you might be invited to come and live with us. If I am not settled, I shall ask him if we can have the dower house. I'm not sure of all the details, but somehow we shall end up with a home of our own."

"You must not refuse to marry on my account."

"I won't, I won't, but you must not worry that I shall end up with no place to go. But right now I want to go to bed for half an hour, if you'll excuse me?"

"Of course, my dear, it has been a trying afternoon."

Instead of ringing for her abigail, Tabitha sank onto her chaise longue. She was close to tears, thinking of the separation so heartlessly engendered by her aunt. It was not easy to forgive her, but it was also far too late to blame her—nine years too late. And to be truthful, she could not have married with her siblings so dependent and suffering the loss of both parents. It had taken much longer than their year of mourning for her father to restore James and Laura's spirits, and so very soon after that their mother had died as well.

But letters from Lord Ashton, even if they had not led to anything, would have been a welcome relief from the daily round. Maybe it was for the best. She had lost her love—if she'd ever had him—when life was at its most difficult, and distraction from the pain had abounded. Perhaps, even, some of her love for Lord Ashton had been a regret to leave the last part of her carefree girlhood. Had the illusion been sustained by an exchange of letters, the disillusionment which would have come when she learned of his attachment to the lady he made his wife would have been all the more hurtful.

Poor Aunt Ellen, imagining she would be making amends by marrying her to Lord Marlton. Thank heavens she had nipped that scheme in the bud. Tabitha shivered, and wrapped a shawl around her shoulders.

There was something singularly repulsive in the gaze Lord Marlton had kept on her. Indeed, she had been seized by the odd fancy that he might want to acquire her as he had acquired his paintings. If he did so, what would he then do?

She wondered about his first marriage. Had his wife regretted her husband's magnanimous gesture? She found herself unwilling to speculate further.

=10=

"IMAGINE, WE'RE GOING TO the opera tonight!" Laura's eyes were gleaming. "Are you not excited, Tabitha?"

Tabitha would have given anything to refuse Lord Marlton's invitation, which had come only a day after their visit to his house, begging them to be his guests at the opera on Tuesday next.

Unfortunately, as Miss Parry had pointed out, they had no engagement that night, and they could hardly refuse an invitation because of an offer of marriage Tabitha had not yet received.

Laura, unaware of her sister's feelings, had expressed such delight at the prospect of hearing the opera, an entertainment she had never witnessed, that Tabitha tried to find pleasure in that. After all, Laura had been very well behaved for several days, and deserved, Tabitha thought, a treat.

"I understand it is a new work," she told her younger sister now.

"Laura, my dear," Miss Parry said, coming into the drawing room and smiling at her niece. "I have seldom seen you in such looks!"

"It is a color that suits me," Laura preened, obviously in agreement with her aunt's encomium.

She did look lovely, Tabitha thought. She was wearing a pink silk gown simply cut, and it seemed to add color to her normally pale complexion. There was a radiance about her that would undoubtedly attract many a masculine eye.

Tabitha hoped that one of those eyes would not belong to Lord Marlton. If he turned his attention from her to her sister, Laura might well decide that she preferred the sure knowledge of being the Lady Marlton to the chance of being Lady Ashton. Of course, the match could be forbidden, but better the whole disaster avoided.

A little shiver went through her. The idea of seeing Lord Marlton again and in the closeness of a box at the opera distressed her. Furthermore, she had a strong feeling that she would be even more distressed by the time the evening was at an end.

It was a great pity that her aunt's feelings of guilt, regarding the part she had played in discouraging the attentions of Lord Ashton, had resulted in this belated effort at matchmaking.

Perhaps Lord Marlton would commit some offense that would give her an excuse to cut him. Perhaps he would come quickly to the point and she could refuse him.

The opera house was crowded that night with throngs of people eager to hear the new work of the composer, Eduardo Torigi, that was being performed. Entitled *La Venedetta,* it gave promise of being sufficiently dramatic and intensely tragic. So said Lord Marlton with a slight sneer.

Noting his expression, Tabitha remembered how he had looked just like that when she had first seen him on horseback in the park, passing too close to Lady Lydford, Lord Ashton, and her. And, superimposed on that, was the image of the face of the man who had shot her father. Oh, how could Aunt Ellen, how could anyone of refinement, imagine that a woman could live as the wife of a relative of the madman who had killed her father?

She longed to go home, but knew that if she did, she would only repine. Taking a deep breath, she put the unpleasant thought out of her mind and gazed about the opera house. She stiffened as she noted a box almost directly across from their own.

With a slight shock, she recognized Lord Ashton, and then she noticed that Laura's gaze was fixed upon him, too. It seemed to her that her sister was breathing a little faster and there was a flush on her cheeks. The most unwelcome suspicion entered Tabitha's mind. Could Laura's affections, seemingly given to no one, be in fact centered on Lord Ashton, despite the girl's constant avowal that she cared only for his title? It was, Tabitha had to admit, not uncommon for someone to deny that they were in love.

It hardly seemed possible! To her certain knowledge, Laura had seen him no more than twice. And yet, Tabitha had fallen in love with him with little more encouragement. As the curtain rose, she fixed her mind firmly on the stage.

The opera opened with a bevy of peasant maidens improbably clad in silken gowns, and among these she recognized one of the French opera dancers she had seen when she first arrived at their London house.

The girl was marvelously graceful. She seemed to float across the floor. When her dance brought her to that part of the stage which lay directly below Lord Ashton's box, Tabitha noticed the girl glance upward and smile at him before being whirled away.

"That . . . creature," Laura hissed. "Did you ever see anything as bold and brazen?"

Tabitha glanced at Laura and was surprised to find her sister's face flushed and anger in her eyes. The dancers had whirled off the stage, and the tenor was singing. Tabitha found herself oddly elated at their disappearance, and then, much to her subsequent dismay, another glance at Lord Ashton's box showed it was now empty.

In that same moment, she heard a small exclamation of annoyance and, glancing at Laura, found her eyes bright with anger. "So, he is running after opera dancers," she whispered. Tabitha felt her heart pounding in her throat, and to her confusion, tears threatened. "You goose," she whispered to her sister, "he's given up the muslin company."

"How do you know?"

"I'll try to explain later." Tabitha wasn't sure herself,

but suspected, from what Henry had said, that Lord Ashton worried about getting a woman with child.

"What?" Laura hissed.

"I'll tell you later."

"Please do not spoil the singing for everyone," said Miss Parry in a quiet but audible tone.

Tabitha paid little attention to the rest of the first act. The dancing girl was beautiful, and there had been such joy in her movements, a joy that had been reflected in her face. She was young and could enjoy her youth as she, Tabitha, had never been allowed to do, prevented by her aunt's watchful and jealous gaze and by her father's terrible death.

It was wrong and foolish to be envious of a woman whose profession put her character at such grave risk, but Tabitha didn't let that stop her.

As the act ended, she heard Lord Marlton speaking to her aunt. Tabitha wished strongly that she could plead a headache and leave, but that was impossible. She glanced at her host and found his eyes on her—a hard, probing gaze as if indeed he were trying to stare into her brain and divine her thoughts!

Fortunately, at that moment Laura said, "Can we go see Lord Ashton? He has returned to his box." She was craning her neck, trying to peer into it.

"I should think not. Laura, sit down. You will give Lord Marlton a disgust of the entire family."

"Never," he protested. "But you had best stay here. What did you think of your first opera?"

"The dancers were very pretty. I think the gentlemen much admire them."

"Yes," Lord Marlton said coldly. "It is the custom for some young and not so young sprigs of the nobility to trifle with these dancing girls. I have never found it attractive to do so. They have the charm of a will-o'-the-wisp and as much staying power. In common with the mayfly, they are dead in a day."

"Yes," Laura nodded, adding spitefully, "and so they should be."

"Laura, my dear," Miss Parry murmured reprovingly, "that is hardly the sort of sentiment you should be expressing, nor is this a subject a girl of your age should discuss."

Laura stared at her coldly and defiantly. "I imagine, Aunt Ellen, that I am only saying what the rest of you are thinking. You know an opera dancer caused Papa's death. And that of Lord Marlton's cousin."

How had the girl come by that bit of unsavory knowledge?

Lord Marlton laughed. "Well said, Lady Laura! I am in complete agreement. Their life is generally short, but what havoc they create whilst they flit about."

As she listened to these comments, Tabitha longed to give her sister a sharp set-down, but with Lord Marlton encouraging her, what could she do? Miss Parry seemed, for once, speechless.

In desperation, Tabitha asked Lord Marlton his opinion of the first act, and found that as usual a gentleman was most willing to air his views. That he now made her his partner in the conversation was a small price to pay for turning the conversation away from her father's death.

The scent of roses permeated the drawing room of the house on Grosvenor Square. There were no less than five bouquets of roses in shades from pink to deep yellow to white arranged in crystal vases. They had been sent by some of the several young bucks of the ton who had earlier visited Laura, eyeing her delightedly and turning hostile glances on their arriving or departing rivals.

Tabitha, sitting in that same chamber some four hours later, could wish those young men were still present. Unfortunately, only Miss Parry was with her. They were awaiting Lord Marlton, who had asked if he might come at five in the afternoon—an hour the chimes of the clock had acknowledged some five minutes since.

"He is late," Miss Parry commented.

Tabitha nodded, praying that he would not come at all. "He—" she began, and paused as the butler threw open the drawing-room door, saying, "Lord Marlton, ma'am."

As usual, he was dressed in the height of fashion. There were gold fobs at his waist and he wore a gold ring with a carved ruby on the middle finger of his right hand. The jewelry was, Tabitha thought disdainfully, far too flamboyant. They surprised her. Generally, he wore only a seal ring. The sight of these additions added to the depression she had been experiencing all day, and which increased at his warm smile as he strode to her side and lifted her hand to his lips to press far too lingering a kiss upon it. She had a strong feeling that he was anticipating an immediate and affirmative answer.

Elation was in his gaze as he said, "Good afternoon, Lady Tabitha."

"Good afternoon, sir." She forced a smile.

He bowed in the direction of Miss Parry. "Good afternoon, ma'am."

"Good afternoon, my lord," she responded.

Tabitha was pleased to have reached the age of twenty-seven. That gave her confidence.

Lord Marlton cleared his throat. "Lady Tabitha," he said in a low voice, "our acquaintance has not been a long one, but I do wish to tell you that from the moment I first saw you, I knew I loved you. I had never imagined myself falling prey to this emotion. I beg that you will do me the honor of becoming my wife."

Tabitha found herself caught by his eyes—a gaze which demanded rather than sought her acquiescence. Anger surged through her. She was aware of a strong impulse to give him an immediate and harsh refusal, but a flock of second thoughts settled upon her like so many stinging bees.

If he were indeed to begin to pursue Laura, and their unpleasant conversation at the opera suggested that he was very aware of her vivaciousness, it might be better not to give him a flat refusal at this time, but wait until Laura was settled.

She said, "I am much honored by your offer, my lord, but I would prefer not to give you an answer at this time."

She paused, hearing a slight gasp from her aunt, but she determinedly continued. "If I might be allowed to think it over, I would be most grateful. Could I give you an answer at the end of the Season?" She knew as she said it, she was asking for too much. It would sound as if she wanted to keep him in reserve in case she did not get a better offer.

There was a pause before he replied, in an oddly muted tone of voice, "I had hoped . . . but no matter . . ." He forced a smile. "I will continue to hope that your answer, when it comes, will be in the affirmative. However, I beg leave to address you again, sooner than you have asked." He rose swiftly. "I must take my leave."

"Then I will bid you good afternoon, my lord," Tabitha said, conscious of the sudden diminishing of a depression she had hardly acknowledged, even to herself. He bowed over her hand once more, his eyes downcast.

She herself was hard put not to smile and indeed laugh and dance for joy. For the moment, she was safe from his attentions and persistent company. And, unless her fancy that he might court her sister was just that, an empty fantasy, so too was Laura safe from the as yet undefined fear which Tabitha felt of Lord Marlton.

=11=

ANOTHER DAY, ANOTHER ROUT—the pattern of their lives was becoming singularly monotonous, Tabitha thought as she came down the stairs to join her aunt in the drawing room. She was, she thought, actually envious of Laura, to whom routs, dinners, and dances were still happily unfamiliar. The thought of one or two or all on any given day was marvelously new to her sister, and she entered gaily into the spirit of every occasion. A little too gaily, was her aunt's often expressed sentiment.

"Your sister, is, I begin to believe, a heartless coquette," Miss Parry had confided to Tabitha several days after Lord Marlton's proposal. "And you, my dear, are hardly better. It is most unkind of you to keep Lord Marlton dangling after your answer. I thought you had quite made up your mind to refuse him."

"I have not heard from him for the better part of a week," she replied. "Consequently, I would hardly say that he is dangling after my answer."

"He is very properly giving you time to consider it," Miss Parry said. "Undoubtedly, he will be present at Lady Abingdon's rout today. I doubt he will pursue that question then, but he will be thinking of it, looking for an indication of your answer in your manner. And he may hint."

Tabitha frowned. Lady Abingdon's rout was to take place that very day, and she was dolefully positive that her aunt's prophecy would come true, at least one aspect of it. Lord Marlton would be present. Still, she hoped against hope that he would not renew his offer at this time. Indeed, it would be difficult, given the way conversation at these affairs battered at the ears. It was generally almost impossible to hear oneself think, and she was reasonably sure that this rout would not be immeasurably different.

"I wish I understood what you were doing, my dear," Miss Parry said plaintively.

Tabitha thought of trying to explain to her aunt her fear that Lord Marlton wanted to marry her because of, not in spite of, the connection between them and that if he could not have her he would want to marry Laura. Then she thought better of it.

As Tabitha had anticipated, the rout, held in the great withdrawing room of Lady Abingdon's mansion on Berkeley Square, appeared to be no different from the others she had attended. There were several new faces and, as usual, she exchanged meaningless comments with recent acquaintances and with a few she had known when first she came to London.

She did have one welcome surprise when Daphne Doncaster, whom she had met at her Presentation at court that first Season Tabitha had spent in London, hurried to her side and greeted her with extreme enthusiasm, her plain face alight with pleasure.

"Tabitha! I just heard tonight you were back in London. How could I have missed it? Oh, my dear, I have so wondered what ever happened to you, vanishing into thin air as you seemed to do between one day and the next!"

"Not into thin air, my dearest Daphne." Tabitha smiled. "Derbyshire. My father . . ." She hesitated.

Her friend's smile vanished. "Oh, my dear, and I not being able to offer my condolences in person, being in Brighton when it happened."

"I do recall your kind letter." Tabitha did remember it, for it was one of the few that made no reference, oblique or otherwise, to the circumstance of her father's death, merely offered what comfort the writer could give to a young woman losing her parent.

"But I never kept up the correspondence," Daphne said sadly, "though I have thought of you so often—every time I see a cat. You must call on me or I will call on you . . . we are at 19 Grosvenor Square."

Tabitha looked at her with pleased surprise. "Opposite Sterling House? What a lovely coincidence."

"Yes, I know. How could we reside just across the square and have only just seen each other, but then I suppose that if we went out at different times—and returned at different times, of course—that we might never have seen each other. And to think I only just heard you were back! Well, that must be immediately rectified!"

"Yes, it certainly shall be," Tabitha agreed warmly.

Daphne shook her head. "It is unpardonable of me not to have called on you . . . you must forgive me, because I never knew you were there . . . And I'll forgive you, if you like. Oh, Lion, my dear," she cried as Lord Ashton came to stand beside her. "You do know Lady Tabitha . . . but, of course, you do, you were such an admirer of her."

"I do, and I was, and I am still." He had been looking rather grave, but then he smiled at Tabitha. He took her proffered hand and bowed over it. "Well met by sunlight, fair Tabitha," he murmured.

"Oh!" Daphne said. "That is from *A Midsummer Night's Dream* . . . or is it that one about whatever you will? . . . though I thought they met by moonlight . . . and outside, in a wood, surely . . . she does look rather like Titania, does she not . . . and she is even more beautiful than when I first knew her. Do you not agree?"

He regarded Tabitha gravely. "Yes, I am quite in agreement with you. Good afternoon, Lady Tabitha."

"Good afternoon, my lord." Tabitha felt warmth on her cheeks and much to her annoyance knew she must be blushing.

"Gracious," gasped Daphne, "do I see Mrs. Stratton? I do . . . and she is glaring at me! I must hurry and greet her, else she will tell my grandmother that I cut her or some such foolishness. Remember, Tabitha, number 19 . . . you will please . . . or I will call . . . but we must see each other, my dearest, we have years and years and years to catch up on—yes, and my name is Fitzroy now."

Before Tabitha could reply, Daphne had dashed away and she was left to face Lord Ashton. She flushed and said, "I have not seen Lady Daphne for such a long time, and, can you imagine, we are living right opposite each other! Do you know her husband, my lord?"

"A coincidence I am sure she will appreciate," he commented. "I do know Mr. Fitzroy. And now, may I be allowed to tell you that you are looking very beautiful this afternoon?"

She made herself look up at him. "You are kind to say so, my lord."

"No, my dear Lady Tabitha, I deny the kindness. I am being entirely truthful."

Again, there was warmth on her cheeks, but she managed to say coolly enough, "I must believe that you are waxing extravagant, my lord."

"No, I assure you, I am not," he said, the slight bantering note she had earlier discerned absent from his voice. "It is the truth, and here, my dear, is another truth. I have come to detest routs, but this one has been made entirely bearable by your presence.

"Before you accuse me of extravagance again, let me assure you that I am not one who cares for artifice, nor do I choose to pay fulsome compliments to females, though I have, of course, done so. Which of us has not yielded to these empty artifices? However, those whom I respect, receive only the truth from me, as sincerity is the greatest compliment I can give them. I have never been other than sincere with you, Lady Tabitha."

"Oh, my lord," she said breathlessly, and wondered what sort of sensible answer she could make to that.

"Ah, Lady Tabitha and Lion." Their hostess surged up to them, her broad face beaming as she gazed at Lord Ashton. "My dear Lion, I have been searching for you everywhere. How does it get so crowded?" She paused, and Tabitha wonder if she expected an answer.

"I rather imagine that you invited a lot of people," offered Lord Ashton.

"I suppose so. When I ask myself that question I receive no answer. Now why did I come here? Oh, yes, Major Sir Thomas Reade. He is your friend, I know."

"Oh, indeed he is. Is he present?" Lord Ashton asked in some surprise. "I thought he was still at home."

"No, he has just arrived. I told him that you would be among my guests. He is across the room near the window. He cannot move from his chair, as I think you probably know. His wounds from Waterloo were grave."

"Oh, yes, I do know." Lord Ashton looked concerned. He turned to Tabitha. "I must see him. He is a very old friend. May I ask leave to take you with me and present him to you, Lady Tabitha?"

"I would be delighted," she answered honestly, happy that she had decided to allow herself the pleasure of being in love with him.

Lord Ashton took her arm and guided her across the crowded room. Sir Thomas was sitting in a wheeled chair, with one or two gentlemen talking to him. When Lord Ashton came up, they waited just long enough to be introduced to Tabitha, then excused themselves.

Tabitha began to suspect from this that she was intruding on the reunion of old friends, and was about to excuse herself when Sir Thomas sent Lord Ashton to find her a chair. "It takes too long to clear a path to wheel me over to an empty one," he explained.

When Lord Ashton was gone, he said, "You must excuse my not getting up for you, Lady Tabitha, but since I cannot rise to the occasion, then I must ask you to sit, for I long to be eye to eye with beauty."

"And I with gallantry," she replied, truthfully. Sir Thomas looked weak and drawn, and Tabitha would not have been surprised to learn that he was in pain. But his eyes were bright and merry in a once handsome face, and his smile was that of a sweet and charming boy, though

Tabitha found his age rather hard to judge. She guessed him a contemporary of Lord Ashton, though there could be five years difference in their ages, with either one of them the elder.

"I find that one of the compensations of my present condition is that, since I cannot pursue the ladies, they must perforce come to me. And since they realize that I cannot chase after them, they are willing to listen to the most outrageous flirting."

"It seems rather shameless of you to take advantage of their kindness, sir," Tabitha replied in a teasing tone. "Were you to be honest, you might quickly learn which ladies truly admired you and which were merely enjoying the flattery. For it is most enjoyable flattery."

"But in your case, Lady Tabitha, I do not need to flatter. Ah, thank you, Ashton," he said as his friend returned with a footman carrying a chair for Tabitha.

Tabitha sat with the gentlemen for a few minutes, then stood, saying, "I cannot tell you, Sir Thomas, how pleased I am to have met you, but I must beg your pardon and go in search of my aunt. She finds these parties delightful but exhausting, and will wish to leave soon."

"You must let me escort you, my lady," said Lord Ashton.

"No, I cannot part two newly reunited friends, for I collect that you have not seen each other for some time."

"That is true," said Sir Thomas. "I came up to town only two days ago, and this is the first time I have ventured out. I do have a promise from Ashton that he will dine with me tomorrow, however, so I could spare him for a few moments." He took Tabitha's hand. "Allow me to say, my dear Lady Tabitha, how much pleasure I have found in meeting one whose name was once so often on my friend's lips. It recalls to me my youth. I hope we shall meet again, and very soon."

Tabitha and Lord Ashton were unable to find Miss Parry in the crowd. When Tabitha spotted several of her aunt's friends gossiping together, she asked Lord Ashton to take her to them. One lady informed her that Miss Parry was indeed looking for her, and Tabitha prevailed upon Lord Ashton to leave her there, while he strolled about searching for Miss Parry.

"It would be very silly for both of us to be walking about looking for each other and constantly passing to the other side of the room without finding each other," Tabitha said. "If she passes this way, I can call out to her, and if she is elsewhere, you will surely send her to me."

With a bow to the ladies and a spoken hope that he would see Lady Tabitha soon again, he took his leave.

"I hope so, too," she could not keep herself from replying, nor could she keep her eyes from him as he made his way across the crowded chamber.

Tabitha stepped a little apart from Miss Parry's friends so that the old ladies might continue to gossip freely, unrestrained by the possibility that a younger and unmarried woman might overhear them. The room was very warm, and she wished that she had a fan with her.

"Might I ask why you are encouraging Lord Ashton, Lady Tabitha?" asked an irate voice.

Recognizing it, Tabitha turned to face a frowning Lord Marlton. Noting his expression, she was angry in turn. "I do not believe I understand you, my lord."

He released a long hissing breath. "I expect that as you are relatively new to the city, you are not aware of his . . . reputation?"

Fury swelled her throat, and it was on the tip of her tongue to give him a set-down he would not soon forget. However, this was not the place to do it, she reminded herself hastily. She said civilly, albeit very coolly, "Lord Ashton is an old friend of mine, my lord. I have known him off and on for nearly nine years."

"May I tell you," he said in a low, angry tone of voice, "that he can be no woman's friend. His reputation as far as females are concerned is of the worst. Did you not see him ogling his *cher ami* at the opera the other night?"

"That, my lord, is no concern of mine, and I might add that you have no jurisdiction over whom I know or with whom I choose to converse." She wondered if Lord

Marlton was maliciously lying to her, or if Henry had misled her as to the character of Lord Ashton.

His eyes narrowed, and it seemed for a moment that he was on the brink of a fiery denunciation. Then he took a long breath. The glare faded from his eyes as he said, "You . . . must forgive me, Lady Tabitha. I was not aware that you were acquainted with Lord Ashton. I cannot believe that—but I will not refine upon the unsavory subject longer. May I hope, dear Lady Tabitha, that you will forgive me for speaking out of concern for a friend I hope to know for many more years than nine?"

She would have given much to withhold that forgiveness—but that might result in further supplication. So she said calmly, "Of course, my lord."

"You are very kind," he said in a low voice. "I think you are aware of how very much I hold you in esteem, but this, alas, is hardly the time to say all that is in my heart. I may, I trust, come to see you at a later date and say, once again, all that is in my heart?"

Again, she was strongly tempted to deny him permission to call, but she was in no mood to start an argument in such a public place. "Of course, my lord."

He caught her hand and, carrying it to his lips, pressed a long kiss on it. "I shall live until that day when I can claim you as my very own, my beautiful Lady Tabitha." Turning, he hurried out of the room, leaving Tabitha shaken and most perturbed.

"My dear." Miss Parry came to her side a moment later. "I just saw Lord Marlton. He looked most concerned. What passed between you?"

"I would prefer to discuss it later, Aunt Ellen," she said. "Indeed, if you are ready to leave, I should not mind going at once."

"I doubt your sister would agree, surrounded as she is by young men."

"Where is she? I do not even see her." Tabitha glanced around the room.

"No more do I," Miss Parry frowned. "Come, let us look

for her together. I expect she is with Pamela. She spent so much time at that girl's house. Ah, there she is in that corner and who—no, I do not believe it!"

"What do you not believe, Aunt Ellen?" Tabitha asked with some consternation.

"Who is that young man with his arm around Laura?"

At that moment Laura must have seen Miss Parry and Tabitha approaching, for she said something to the young man next to her, whose arm was indeed around her waist. He let go of her immediately and set off in the opposite direction to Miss Parry and Lady Tabitha. As he departed hastily, Tabitha caught a glimpse of his face. It was, she saw with much consternation, Sir Frederick Perdue.

=12=

"WELL, THEN?" HAVING SPENT an angry hour admonishing a seething Laura, then sending her to her chamber, Miss Parry regarded Tabitha nervously. "What, pray, went amiss with you this afternoon?"

"I cannot like Lord Marlton," Tabitha said, mildly, hoping to avoid further upsetting her aunt.

She had refrained from mentioning to her aunt that the man whom Laura had permitted to be so very familiar was Sir Frederick. She planned to task her sister with the knowledge later, and to make it clear to Laura that she was to avoid him in the future. If necessary, she would even involve Henry, although she dreaded trying to make him be firm with Laura.

He was more likely to call Sir Frederick out. That would only bring to a head the very scandal that Tabitha so wished to prevent.

Miss Parry raised her eyes to heaven. "Oh, dear, was he rude? I cannot imagine it of him. I know that you do not want me to encourage his suit, but he is besotted with you, and very rich, and well-born."

"I beg you will not cite his wealth and his position. There are other qualifications he does not possess—what he does possess in amazing amounts is impertinence."

"Impertinence?" Miss Parry echoed. "That term is better suited to a recalcitrant lackey."

"He was impertinent!" Tabitha's good intentions were

forgotten. She rose and took a turn around the drawing room, coming to stand in front of her aunt. "I call it impertinent and interfering for him to dare to tell me with whom I should and should not converse!"

Miss Parry gazed at her in some surprise. "Did he do such a thing?"

"He did. He noticed me talking with Lord Ashton and saw fit to warn me about his wild ways as if I were Laura's age or even younger. And I do not believe that Lord Ashton is wild at all. If he was, Henry would be in his pocket, and I see no evidence that they are cronies."

Miss Parry nodded. "Well, my dear, it was rather high-handed of Lord Marlton, but—"

"I prefer to say it was impertinent!" Tabitha started to pace.

"Come and sit next to me, my dear," Miss Parry said, "you are making my head ache. I suppose I should lay that at Laura's door, but you still add to the pain by moving about."

Tabitha obeyed. "I am sorry, Aunt Ellen, I don't know why I am so annoyed with him."

"The man, my dear, is deeply in love with you," her aunt explained.

"And therefore imagines he has the right to exercise jurisdiction over me? I think not!" Tabitha said, keeping her voice low.

"My dear, you must take into account that men in love are often extremely jealous . . . and he is in love with you, very deeply in love, I should say. That is obvious."

A pleading note had crept into Miss Parry's voice. "My dear, think well before you make a decision. And pray remember what I have told you—if you want to marry, do so quickly. It is your good fortune to have lost nothing in looks. Indeed, I think you might be even more beautiful than you were at eighteen . . . And with Lord Marlton, you would have wealth and position. Is that not more to your liking than spending the rest of your life as an unpaid chaperone?"

"I think . . . ," Tabitha said slowly, "that any woman

would rather be in that position than married to someone she did not like."

"You are so dramatic. You have not given yourself a chance to like him. You have not seen him often. Please, my dear, do not make any irrevocable decision as yet."

Tabitha suddenly felt very sorry for her aunt, whom she knew was deeply regretting her earlier interference between herself and Lord Ashton and was still trying to make amends, but she was positive that she would never be able to accept Lord Marlton's offer. The very sight of him repelled her.

"Aunt Ellen," she said, " nothing you can say will make me change my mind, but if you are determined to see me wed, let us make up a list of suitors more pleasing to both of us."

"Well, my dear," said Miss Parry, "it had best be a gentleman in a hurry to wed, for if you are not settled by the time you are eight-and-twenty, I would not recommend marriage. Unless, of course, to a man who already had heirs, who wanted a mother for them, rather than a companion for himself." She colored. "I trust you are old enough to understand what I mean?"

"But I should enjoy a family of my own," Tabitha said, "so let us concentrate on hasty gentlemen."

"You realize," said Miss Parry, who always felt a need to make everything painfully clear, "that this precludes Lord Ashton, for he shows no sign of wishing to remarry."

"Then," said Tabitha as lightly as she could, "we shall strike him from the list!"

After a half hour of listening to Miss Parry weigh the relative merits of various gentlemen of their acquaintance, Tabitha decided she had humored her aunt long enough, and excused herself to dress for dinner.

As she rang the bell for Jane, she reflected on how thankful she was that she had turned Miss Parry's mind from Lord Marlton. She shivered, extremely pleased that she could dictate, albeit in a gentle and often indirect manner, to her aunt. There was, it seemed, more than one compensation in having reached the age of twenty-seven!

Once Tabitha was dressed, she went to see Laura, who was to have her dinner on a tray in her room. When Laura had protested against this childish punishment, Miss Parry had said that she was lucky she was not whipped. Laura, conscious that none of her doting relatives had ever struck her, had laughed.

When Tabitha had scratched on the door of her sister's bedchamber, and been bidden to enter, she found Laura sitting by the window. She was scribbling on a piece of paper, which, as her sister came in, she screwed into a ball and tossed into the empty grate.

"So, have you come to ring another peal over my head?" she asked crossly.

"Yes, I have." Tabitha sat down, facing her sister. "I saw that you were with Sir Frederick this afternoon. I have not told Aunt Ellen."

"Do me no favors, sister," said Laura. "I am not afraid of her."

"It is for her sake, not yours, that I kept silent." Tabitha could imagine her poor aunt's reaction to the news that the man Laura had once tried to elope with was restored to her niece's favor. This time, perhaps, Miss Parry really would not be able to cope. "I am no longer willing to be amused by your antics, Laura. I have very little to say, save that you will not leave my side in company except to dance, and you will make sure that you are escorted back to me or Aunt Ellen. If you see Sir Frederick, you will not approach him. If he comes up to us, you will say nothing, even if he addresses you. You will let me speak to him, and you will follow my lead. If I say we are tired and about to leave, you will not contradict me."

"And if I am with Aunt Ellen—after one of the men you will so generously allow me to dance with has returned me to her?" Laura demanded. "I do not think this is such a good idea, Tabitha, for you cannot keep me on leading strings."

"If you are with Aunt Ellen, you will keep silent and obey her. If you do not, I shall tell her that you were with him, use that as a reason for having her forbid you to leave the house, and I shall write to William and have him come to take you home. That will be the end of your Season, and I very much doubt that you will be permitted another.

"I could explain to you again why your actions are so foolish, but if you did not understand Aunt Ellen's explanation earlier, then there is no point in my trying. And I am not jesting with you, Laura. Behave yourself, or we will return to Derbyshire forthwith. Believe me, it would be a pleasure for Aunt Ellen and me."

For once Laura had no answer to make.

"My dearest Tabitha," Lady Daphne Fitzroy, sitting on the sofa beside her friend, said warmly. "I was so sorry you left early yesterday, but then I remembered that I could easily see you again and here I am . . . I hope I am not too early?" She glanced rather guiltily at the clock on the mantelpiece. "It is no more than a quarter after ten, but your note did say that you would welcome an informal call at any time. And since you were awake enough to dispatch a note, I could only hope you were awake enough to receive me."

"I would have been as glad to see you as I am now to see you had you arrived at nine o'clock or eight or seven," Tabitha said warmly.

"Oh, dear, I could never flout convention to that extent," said Lady Daphne. "Have I told you that you look quite ravishing? I would never dare wear light blue . . . but you are so divinely slim. Of course, I was slim before I married dearest Samuel. In fact, one of his first remarks to me when we met at a ball somewhere . . . or perhaps it was an assembly at Almack's . . . anyway, he said that I looked like a sylph or a naiad, or something slender and classic . . . well, he didn't say all that . . . just that I looked like one of them . . . and so did he! He was slim as a reed, and now he has a double chin! He says that marriage has ruined him. He is kind enough to add that it has ruined both of us, but actually it is really the fault of Monsieur Tibault!"

"Monsieur Tibault?" Tabitha questioned as Lady Daphne paused for breath. Her friend's conversational manner had not changed with marriage. She still made breathless starts at a topic, then ended up speaking about something completely different, leaving her listener at a loss to follow her.

"Our chef . . . it is de rigueur to have a French chef, as I am sure you are aware . . . and by a great stroke of luck we discovered him in Paris while we were on our honeymoon."

"Paris, you went to Paris . . . how lovely," Tabitha said, picking out a single fact to reply to.

"Well, it was, but only briefly. We had to leave in the most extreme rush . . . because that horrid little man had slipped his chain in Elba and was on the march again. Monsieur Tibault, learning of our decision, practically fell on his knees . . . or would have had he not been so fat . . . and with tears in his eyes, he begged us to take him with us . . . he being of royalist sympathies . . . and such a good cook, too." Lady Daphne sighed heavily.

"Such a crossing as we had," she continued. "The boat was absolutely crammed with all us craven English . . . poor Samuel and the other men were on the deck all night . . . though it is not really craven to want not to be thrust into a French prison . . . because as Samuel said, we would have caused too much trouble effecting our release . . . and guillotined, or perhaps they would only have starved us. I do not know . . . for I don't suppose Monsieur Tibault could cook in prison.

"But we did get away and Monsieur Tibault is still with us . . . even though I cannot tell you the number of guests who have partaken of our dinners and subsequently tried to steal him . . . well, entice him for more money even though we pay him well . . . because stealing him would be slavery . . . and he is French. However, he has never budged from our kitchen except to sleep and buy food . . . he gets up at dawn to buy the freshest . . . and furthermore, he has married our housekeeper which, I think, has helped ensure his loyalty."

"I imagine that he would be loyal in any circumstance," Tabitha said. "You did save his life."

"Oh, anyone would have helped him . . . especially if they had tasted his cooking. But he does seem to be loyal . . . he has the gift of loyalty and that is a real gift. By the way, did I see you conversing with Lord Marlton?"

"Yes, you did. Are you acquainted with him?" Tabitha wondered how loyalty led to Lord Marlton in Lady Daphne's muddled mind.

"We have—met." There was a slight frown on Daphne's brow. "Samuel knows him, though I cannot say they are friends. Now, Lord Ashton is quite another story . . . such a charming man, do you not agree? But, of course, you must . . . I can remember you dancing with him at Almack's all those years ago . . . at least he was your partner in the cotillion and the quadrille . . . is it not a pity we were forbidden to waltz in those days? I do love a waltz, do not you?"

"Oh, yes, I do," Tabitha said, remembering the one waltz she had been able to give Lord Ashton at Almack's. "I am glad that the patronesses at Almack's now allow it."

"Yes, finally . . . they are such sticklers for propriety, even though their own characters . . . I suppose you have been told that the Countess de Lieven . . . and she seems so nice. I do wish people were more like themselves . . . if you understand me . . . then people like Lord Marlton could not confuse us."

"What about Lord Marlton?" Tabitha asked.

"Oh, his poor little wife . . . her father, Lord Lassiter, was a great friend of your papa . . . and after . . . well, when all that unpleasantness happened . . . Lord Lassiter told everyone that it served Lord Marlton's cousin right . . . dying by his own hand. So, then Lord Lassiter died . . . and poor little Phoebe was left without a penny . . . and Lord Marlton was very kind to her and she married him . . . and then every time they went out in public . . . and he took her everywhere . . . he said cruel things about her. I expect she was glad when she found she was expecting a child and could retire from

Society . . . the poor little thing's in the country now . . . and he hardly ever goes there."

"I thought Lady Marlton died," Tabitha said, pleased to be at last getting some information about Lord Marlton's character from someone who would not attribute her interest to a motive relating to marriage.

"Oh, she did . . . he made her come back to London soon after the baby was born . . . she missed her child dreadfully . . . that's who's in the country . . . and then a year later she fell ill and died. . . . I think he was even more unkind to her in private than he was in public . . . he'd say the most cutting things to her . . . but she always seemed reluctant to leave a gathering . . . and—" Daphne paused as the butler appeared in the doorway.

"Yes, James?" Tabitha said.

"If you please, milady, Lord Marlton has arrived and wishes to see you."

"Very well. And will you please inform Miss Parry and ask if she would please join us, James?"

"Yes, your ladyship." The butler nodded and withdrew.

"Oh, dear." Daphne rose hastily. "I must be going . . . or would you like protection?"

"No, thank you, Daphne, I shall be fine." She didn't want to be constrained in her refusal of Lord Marlton by the presence of someone outside the family.

"Well . . . if you are certain. . . . I haven't asked after Miss Parry, or your sister, or your very handsome brother . . . everyone wishes *he* were not married . . . and I didn't tell you about my baby . . . you must come and see the heir apparent."

"I should be delighted to see him." Tabitha smiled. "I expect he's talking already, even if he's still a babe in arms."

Tabitha bade her chattering friend farewell, and sat down, in a chair, to preclude having to share a sofa, to await Lord Marlton. Now that her opinion of him and his marriage was confirmed, she planned to refuse him firmly. Lady Daphne always prattled on, but she generally told you only what she had observed, for she rarely had time to listen to anyone else's opinions.

The butler appeared once more to say in his sonorous tones, "Lord Marlton, milady."

Lord Marlton came quickly into the chamber. He was smiling, and once he had taken her hand in greeting, he seemed reluctant to let it go.

"Will you not sit down, my lord?" she asked, gesturing to the sofa.

"I thank you," he said stiffly and took a chair far too near hers. He added, "I did not know you were acquainted with Lady Daphne. I passed her in the hall. I hope I did not interrupt, but I did not expect to find anyone calling so early."

"Lady Daphne has been my friend for many years, my lord, and in such circumstance formality may be relaxed. We met when first I came to London."

"She is indeed fortunate," he said. "I would I might have had the pleasure of meeting you then, but I cannot like you being friends with her." He rose hastily as Miss Parry hurried into the chamber. "Good morning, ma'am." He bowed.

"Good morning, Lord Marlton," she said and smiled graciously as he shook hands. "Will you not be seated, my lord?" she invited.

"Thank you, ma'am," he said, politely waiting until she had taken a seat on the sofa before returning to his chair. He added, "The reason I arrived so early is that I have been called out of town. I am not sure how long I shall be gone." He fastened an eager gaze on Tabitha's face. "But when I return, I pray you will have made your decision and can give me the happy answer I crave."

Tabitha longed to shout she would not, could not, marry him, if he were the last man on earth. Now at last she could say no. She realized that there was no longer any reason to protect Laura: her sister would never dream of marrying a man so dictatorial. And now that she had Laura more firmly under control, she did not have to worry about the possibility of Laura kicking up a fuss over denying Lord Marlton's suit.

She replied in her firmest tone, "I am sensible of the honor you do me, sir, but I feel that we could not suit. I must, and do, decline your proposal of marriage."

"Oh, my dear, I have been too precipitous. You cannot know so quickly if we are compatible. When I return to town, I shall call again, and often. My cousin and I shall invite you and your family to dinner. We shall spend much time in each other's company, and then, and only then, will I ask you again." He rose. "I must go. I will bid you farewell."

Tabitha, also rising, refrained from offering her hand. "Farewell, my lord, but there is no need for you to call again. I fear that I shall never wish to be your wife—"

Lord Marlton interrupted her speech to say, "Good day, Miss Parry," and walked out of the room while Tabitha was still speaking.

For once, Miss Parry was silent. As Tabitha stood there seething, Laura came into the room. "I saw Lord Marlton climbing into his carriage. He was here early."

"Yes, he is leaving town," Tabitha explained, wishing strongly that his lordship were leaving England as well.

"He appears much taken with you," Laura said.

"He *is* much taken with her," Miss Parry said. "Tabitha is not so taken with him."

Tabitha shook her head. "I am not at all taken with him. I shudder to imagine why he wants to marry me. If he did he would put my happiness before his petty desires. I don't imagine any woman would want to marry—"

"Oh, I would," Laura said. "He is extremely wealthy, and I understand from Cornelia Wyndham that he has a magnificent castle in the north."

"Wealth is not everything," Tabitha snapped. "Sanity is."

"If he were insane, he'd be confined," said Laura. "I think that a woman at her last prayers would be very pleased to marry him."

Tabitha wondered if Laura meant to be rude by implication or if she was just being careless in her speech. "Even a woman at her last prayers has some sense, Laura. And there are worse fates than being unwed."

"If I were you, Tabitha . . . ," Miss Parry began. She paused as the butler appeared in the doorway. "Yes, James?" she inquired.

"If you please, ma'am, Lord Ashton has arrived."

"Oh, show him in, James!" Laura cried excitedly.

"Your . . . er, ma'am?" the butler looked questioningly at Miss Parry.

"Yes, James, please show him in," Miss Parry said. Waiting until the butler had left the chamber, she frowned at Laura. "It is hardly your place to issue such orders, my dear. Please try for a little comportment."

"You were not about to turn Lord Ashton away, Aunt Ellen, surely?" Laura regarded her with wide eyes.

"Certainly I was not about to turn him away!" her aunt snapped.

Hearing the excitement in Laura's tone and seeing it reflected in her eyes, Tabitha recalled the suspicions that had been aroused during the performance at the opera the other night. Could her sister really have developed a *tendre* for Lord Ashton? When he entered, she was uncomfortably sure of it. Laura's face was flushed and she appeared quite breathless as he greeted them. Were his eyes lingering on Laura's face or was she mistaken? After all, Lord Ashton had looked at her, too, and at Miss Parry, as he bent to shake her hand.

Why, Tabitha thought unhappily, was she indulging in these speculations? "As he to Hercules . . ." The phrase swept through her mind . . . Hamlet comparing his wicked uncle to his noble father. Her thoughts were scattered, and she fought for control.

Lord Ashton said, "I hope you will pardon my early intrusion. I have come with two invitations."

Smiling at Laura, he said, "My sister is waiting outside with her children on a spontaneous outing to the tower. She recalled that Lady Laura expressed an interest in children, so we stopped by on the chance that you ladies might be free."

He turned to face Tabitha. "And I have an invitation to the theater."

"To the theater!" Laura cried, clapping her hands together. "How exciting, my lord!"

Lord Ashton turned reluctantly back to her, but he smiled politely, "I am in hopes that it will be. Edward Kingsley, whom I knew at Oxford, has written a play called *The Rake's Revenge*. It will be performed at the Haymarket."

"Oh, how very thrilling to know the playwright," Laura said breathlessly.

"He certainly must be extremely talented to have a production at the Haymarket," Tabitha commented. "I take it he is an amateur?"

"Of some note," Lord Ashton replied. "He is very gifted. May I count on your attendance, then?" He smiled at Tabitha.

"Oh, you most certainly may, my lord," Laura assured him. "Thank you for thinking of me, of us. We all enjoy an evening at the theater."

"I would certainly like to see it," Tabitha said, more quietly.

"I do hope you will all be free. It will be a week tomorrow." He took a step toward Tabitha. "Will that be convenient for you, my lady?"

"Oh, yes, we will all be free!" Laura exclaimed. "I can hardly wait! And I do want to go to the tower. Come, Tabitha, we must not keep Lady Lydford waiting."

"And you, ma'am? Are you coming to the tower with us?" Lord Ashton asked Miss Parry.

"No, thank you, my lord," Miss Parry replied. "But I am sure that Tabitha will enjoy it."

"And so shall I. I will fetch your bonnet, Tabitha," Laura called, as she hurried from the room.

=13=

THE DAY WHICH HAD begun badly with Lord Marlton's visit, then improved greatly with an excursion to the Tower of London with Lord Ashton, was fated to end poorly at dinner.

Tabitha had enjoyed herself at the tower very much. Lady Lydford had kept Laura by her side, with the nursemaid and her younger children, leaving Tabitha free to stroll on Lord Ashton's arm.

They'd had no opportunity for private conversation, as Lord Ashton's little niece was with them, clutching Tabitha's hand, but it had been a pleasure to watch him with the child and to take part in a conversation with him that was not dominated by Laura.

Now, the ladies were dining alone, for as usual Henry was at his club. Tabitha brought up *The Rake's Revenge*. "I am looking forward to it," she said. "It does seem strange to think of someone actually sitting down and writing a play. I wonder if he speaks the parts out loud?"

"It is most kind of Lord Ashton to invite us," Miss Parry said. She had no use for, or understanding of, the sort of speculation Tabitha was indulging in.

"Oh!" Laura exclaimed. "Just think—a play, and at the Haymarket. I have been longing to go to the theater again, though it is said to be extremely warm at this time of year. I do like Lord Ashton for asking us."

Miss Parry frowned at her. "It was quite out of the way to put yourself forward as you did this morning, Laura."

Laura gazed at her wide-eyed. "Put myself forward, Aunt Ellen? I do not understand you."

"When he issued his invitation to the theater, Lord Ashton was speaking mainly to your sister."

"Why, that is not true, not in the least," Laura cried. "He looked at all of us!"

"He is your sister's friend," Miss Parry said coolly. "You would do well to remember that."

"And not mine?" Laura questioned. Before Miss Parry could respond, she continued, "He has always been very friendly to me, coming to see me when I was ill. If he is so particularly friendly to Tabitha, it should seem to me that we should have seen more of him, which we have not. I am sure that he has many friends."

"It is still most unseemly for you to put yourself forward in that unbecoming way." Her aunt frowned. "Manners such as these will give people quite a disgust of you."

As she listened to this conversation, Tabitha found herself quite as annoyed with Laura as was Miss Parry. Her sister had hardly let her get a word in edgewise as she boldly monopolized the conversation and Lord Ashton.

She had it in mind to reprimand Laura, but what would have been the use? The girl would pay no more heed to her than she was currently paying to Miss Parry. The only threat that seemed to work was that of removing her from London, and she knew that if she used it too often, Laura would regard it as empty.

But why did Laura have to be so rude in front of Lord Ashton? Because she was attracted to him, regardless of the fact that he must be at least fifteen years older than Laura! Still, such marriages were not unusual. Girls of eighteen or seventeen did wed gentlemen in their forties and fifties—even in their sixties! Furthermore, Laura was beautiful and young. She might well imagine that he would offer for her.

"I think you all hate me," Laura cried unexpectedly. "None of you wants me to be happy!" She ran from the room, and Miss Parry burst into tears.

Tabitha comforted her aunt. For her the day was

spoiled. The ball that night did not cheer her. In order to keep an eye on Laura, she did not dance, and constantly had to assure Miss Parry that while she was a little tired she did not wish to go home.

Lord Ashton, who was also present, was very attentive, but he could hardly spend the whole evening by her side. And, to tell the truth, he did not seem particularly unhappy when she refused him a waltz.

He did not ask Laura to dance, and Tabitha rather expected a show of temper on the way home, but Laura, who with her friends Pamela and Cornelia had enjoyed a triumphant evening, was in a good mood.

The rest of the week passed much the same way. Laura's pleasant manner continued, and Tabitha spent almost every waking moment by her side, except when Laura went to call on Pamela or Cornelia, or when those girls were with her. She, Tabitha, needed a respite sometime, and she felt that Laura would appreciate one too.

The main drawback to this constant chaperonage was the fact that she avoided Lord Ashton as much as possible, even denying him one afternoon when he called. She was alone in the house with Laura and as usual could not face the embarrassment of seeing her little sister throw herself at him in her usual common and rude way.

The best part of the week, as far as Tabitha was concerned, was that Lord Marlton did not come to call. She had written him a cold note, which was, she assumed, either waiting for him in London or had been sent after him. She hoped that after reading it, he would cease his unwelcome pursuit. If that failed, she would write to William and then send Lord Marlton to apply to him.

It would be worth the scold she'd receive from her brother for getting herself into such a pickle—although she knew she was innocent—to have him dismissed as a suitor for her hand by her brother. What a shame a man would accept as truth from another of his own sex what he would not accept from a woman.

Wednesday finally arrived. Tabitha sat at her mirror

while her abigail arranged her hair—hardly able to believe that the long-awaited hour was so close.

"Oh, milady, your hair is like spun gold," Jane murmured, as she arranged it.

"I do believe you wax extravagant, Jane," Tabitha reproved.

"Oh, no, milady. With your gown being so flattering a shade wi' that necklace . . . I've never seen you look better."

"You are very kind to say so, Jane." Tabitha forced a smile, wishing the girl would cease her encomiums and hurry, but finally she was finished and Tabitha arrayed in one of her new gowns, the amber silk she had ordered made for her to wear with the intaglio necklace.

The skirts were slightly fuller than she was accustomed to. The mantua-maker had told her this was the latest fashion. Why was she thinking of fashion? She did not care a fig for the changing styles! Well, she did really, because these new ones were flattering and she did want to be at her best this night.

"Oh, milady, if you do not look a picture," the abigail breathed.

"You flatter me, Jane," Tabitha said reprovingly.

"Oh, milady, I do not. Such lovely hair you have, an' easy to manage, not all flyaway. Not like Lady Laura's. Betsy says that hers be so fine, t'will always escape the combs.

"But my sister's hair is such a lovely color," Tabitha felt it incumbent upon her to say.

"Oh, yes, milady, but I prefer your color, not so white. Now 'tis the intaglio necklace you'll be wantin'?"

"Yes, Jane," Tabitha said softly, remembering that it had a twofold sentimental value, since in addition to being a present from her grandfather, she had worn it on the night she first danced at Almack's and then again at Almack's this Season. Indeed, it was rather like a talisman, she thought. She suddenly remembered her grandfather saying, "Wear it for luck, my dearest."

Lord Ashton arrived promptly. He had brought his carriage and, as Miss Parry, Tabitha, and Laura came to the vehicle, he handed Miss Parry inside and would have helped Laura in, too. But even as he reached for her hand, she moved back to stand behind Tabitha.

"Oh, dear, I have forgotten my reticule. I must go in and fetch it," she exclaimed.

"Gracious, such carelessness," Miss Parry said, reprovingly. "I beg you'll hurry, Laura."

"Oh, I shall. I am so sorry," Laura said. She moved hastily toward the front door while Lord Ashton handed Tabitha into the coach.

A few minutes later, Laura returned, carrying her reticule. "I do hope I was not too long," she said, lifting anxious eyes to Lord Ashton's face.

"No, not in the least, Lady Laura," he assured her as he handed her into the coach. "It was good you found it so quickly."

"I was almost positive I had left it on a chair in the drawing room," she said.

If Tabitha had not caught a note of triumph in Laura's voice, she would have thought nothing of that forgotten reticule. But, hearing that particular cadence and subsequently seeing her sister's small smile as she took her seat beside Lord Ashton, she hardly needed her aunt's little dig in the ribs to see through Laura's stratagem.

Tabitha could have laughed. If Laura had simply been content to be the shy young maiden, she could easily have offered to sit with her back to the horses, leaving her aunt and older sister the forward-facing seat. Her little game with the reticule would only amuse, not impress, Lord Ashton.

Laura made the most of her place by Lord Ashton as the carriage pitched its way through the crowded streets. She was in a questioning mood, asking Lord Ashton about the Haymarket and also about the young playwright. Miss Parry nudged Tabitha once again—a movement that needed no interpretation as Laura, sitting close to Lord Ashton, favored him with one of her most provocative smiles.

*   *   *

"Oh, how lovely," Laura breathed as she came into a box directly over the stage. "We shall be able to see so very well. I should loathe sitting in the pit."

"Both locations have their advantages, I think, though ladies never sit there," Lord Ashton commented. "You and your sister must take the two front chairs."

"I should not mind," Laura said quickly, "if my aunt would prefer the forward seat."

"No, my dearest Laura, but I do thank you for your generosity," Miss Parry said dryly.

"I shall move a chair forward for Miss Parry," Lord Ashton said. "There is no need for you to worry, Lady Laura."

Once they were settled, Lord Ashton, leaning forward, said to Tabitha, "Have I told you that you are in splendid looks tonight?"

Tabitha was certain that her new gown was responsible for the praise. She was about to thank him for a compliment that both surprised and pleased her, but in that same moment, Laura, gazing at a box across the house and situated almost precisely opposite their own, said in a low but excited tone of voice, "Would those ladies over there be Fashionable Impures?" She indicated the box with a flip of her fan.

Lord Ashton glanced in that direction at the same time Miss Parry leaned forward to say crossly, "My dear Laura, a lady does not ask such questions. She does not recognize the existence of such people! For a young lady like yourself, it is highly indelicate."

Laura giggled and turned wide eyes on her aunt. "But everyone knows about them."

"You do not," Miss Parry snapped.

"My friend Pamela says—" Laura began defiantly.

"If that is what you discuss, you may have to find a new friend," Miss Parry interrupted.

Glancing across the house in the indicated direction, Tabitha had a most uncomfortable memory of a similar group of ladies sitting in a box at the opera house—all those years ago. She wished strongly that she had not thought of them. Fortunately for her peace of mind, the curtain rose on the play.

The work was well-staged, well-acted, and very well-written. It concerned the machinations of one Sir Barnaby Shelton, a handsome, but impoverished, ne'er-do-well, as he cruelly laid siege to the heart of the innocent, sheltered daughter of a mild and forgetful nobleman.

The play was quite absorbing, though much to Tabitha's annoyance, her sister was extremely restless, assiduously fanning herself and uttering little gasps of distress.

Consequently, once the curtain fell on the first act, Miss Parry leaned forward to ask impatiently, "Whatever is the matter, Laura?"

"Oh, Aunt Ellen," she moaned. "I . . . I am so very warm. I was afraid I might swoon. I . . . I must have a breath of fresh air."

"I had better take you outside," Lord Ashton said quickly. "It is warm in here. Should you like to come with us, Lady Tabitha?"

"No, thank you, my lord," she said. "I am perfectly comfortable." Tabitha was not sure she could stand the embarrassment of watching Laura's own playacting.

"I, however, will come with you," Miss Parry said decisively. "And Tabitha, my dear, you had best come, too. I don't like to leave you alone in the box."

As they left the house and walked through the lobby, Tabitha looked for someone else she knew in the hopes of attaching herself to their party for the intermission. However, she saw none of her friends or acquaintances close enough to speak to.

On coming out of the theater, Laura drew deep breaths of air. "It is much cooler here. I do thank you for bringing me down. And does not the sky look beautiful tonight? So many stars and the moon almost full." She smiled warmly at Lord Ashton.

"You have your sister's taste." Lord Ashton also smiled. "I recall Lady Tabitha mentioning that she always enjoyed the spread of an evening sky." He looked at Tabitha. "You called it heavenly artistry."

Laura, clinging to Lord Ashton's arm, said, "I doubt if Tabitha's intended would agree with that. I understand that he prefers paintings to—"

"Tabitha's . . . intended?" Lord Ashton interrupted quickly.

"Laura!" Tabitha cried.

Miss Parry added her protest. "Nothing is settled as yet."

"But I am sure it will be." Laura smiled provocatively up at Lord Ashton. "We are delighted at the thought of Tabitha as a bride."

"I wish you would not discuss my private business, Laura," Tabitha said angrily. "I have made up my mind about Lord Marlton's flattering proposal, and I shall give him my answer when he returns." She longed to return to the theater, or even better to go home, but she could not stalk off by herself.

"I think," said Miss Parry, "that we should return to the box. Laura seems fully recovered."

"But to be certain the cure is complete," Lord Ashton said, "I shall leave Lady Laura in Miss Parry's care to slowly make her way to the box. And, if I can beg your company, Lady Tabitha, we shall hurry ahead and you can help me select oranges for your sister. I can never tell which are ripe."

"How very kind of you, my lord." Miss Parry took Laura's hand and tucked it securely in the crook of her own arm. "Lean on me, my dear. If you are overheated, you must be treated as such."

Laura opened her mouth as if to protest, then closed it again. She fluttered her eyelashes, and said, "Oh, my lord, how very sweet of you."

Lord Ashton offered his arm to Tabitha. "My lady?"

Tabitha placed her hand on his arm and they walked away. She was afraid Lord Ashton would make some comment of sympathy for the rejected Lord Marlton, and to forestall it she spoke. "Your friend is—"

At that same moment, Lord Ashton had begun, "My friend is—"

He, too, broke off and they both laughed.

"Your pardon, Lady Tabitha, for interrupting you."

"We spoke together, my lord. And unless I miss my guess, we were both about to praise your friend."

"His work is delightful, is it not?"

Tabitha wished she could think of a more stimulating response than a mere "Yes, indeed."

Lord Ashton sounded nearly as strained as she felt, but he gamely added, "And so very amusing."

When they were inside again, Lord Ashton purchased four oranges from an orange girl, then walked about with Tabitha until Miss Parry and Laura returned.

Once they were all back in their seats, Laura announced that she was feeling much better.

"Yes, the air was quite refreshing." Miss Parry nodded.

Laura turned her attention to Lord Ashton, teasing him as he peeled their oranges with the tiny knife he used as a watch fob.

Tabitha gazed about the house. Earlier in the evening, she had been struck by the fact that their box was in much the same position as that in which she, her father, and her aunt had sat that night nine years ago.

Then, Lord Sterling had gone downstairs during the interval and Lord Ashton—still Lord Lovell—had come to the box and . . . she shuddered, wishing she had not been visited by that most unhappy memory. She must make a strong effort to banish it. Why, indeed, had it reared its ugly head on this night?

She had been to other theaters this season. Was it possible that the presence of Lord Ashton had brought it to mind? She shuddered. She had an instant and most unwelcome memory of her recent visit to the opera with Lord Marlton. She sighed. Lord Ashton offered her a segment of orange.

"Are you even listening?" Laura's voice broke through her thoughts.

"I beg your pardon. What did you say?"

"I said I was better," Laura said in a lilting tone of voice. "It was much cooler outside and I am much refreshed! And I asked if you were."

"I cannot think why you should be," Miss Parry said crossly. "It is almost as warm outside as it is inside. Did you not find it so, my lord?"

"Yes, I must say that I did not find it appreciably cooler than in the theater," he said.

"I think it's much warmer in here," Laura insisted. "In fact . . ." She stopped speaking, for the curtain was rising.

Sitting back in her chair, Tabitha found it nearly impossible to concentrate on what was taking place on stage. She was remembering Lord Ashton's odd expression as he gazed at her. Indeed, there had been questions in his eyes which had not been present when he had left the box, as if indeed she had done something that had displeased him. What could that have been? He had smiled at her warmly as he had escorted her aunt and sister from the box.

Suddenly, her ears were filled with the sound of a shot. In her mind's eye her father's image returned—as he had looked that fatal night, the blood staining his brocade waistcoat.

She screamed.

=14=

"LORD, WHAT A GREAT silly you are," Laura said contemptuously. "It's only the play." She glanced smilingly over her shoulder. "Poor Tabitha, unable to tell the difference between what is real and pretense."

Lord Ashton had risen to his feet. "It is not the play. I am surprised you do not realize that, Lady Laura," he said very coldly. "It is much, much more than the play."

Laura did not heed him. She glared at a still shaken Tabitha. "You are making a great cake of yourself, I must say," she hissed and then stared up in sheer amazement as Lord Ashton, edging to Tabitha's side, drew her gently to her feet and put an arm around her shoulders.

Looking at Miss Parry, he murmured, "I will take Lady Tabitha home and return for you and Lady Laura afterward. If the play ends before I come back, I pray you will still wait here for me."

"We should come with you," Miss Parry whispered as she stood up. "Laura, gather up your cloak, and take your sister's, too."

"Sit down, Tabitha, I don't want to miss the end," Laura said peevishly. "I am certain that you will be all right in a moment."

"Your sister is badly shocked," said Miss Parry. "Surely you recall being told that she was present when your father was shot to death in a theater."

"But I wasn't," said Laura. "I'm going to go to Pamela's box and ask her mama to take me home." She ran out of the box, leaving the door open behind her.

"Oh, do excuse me," said a distraught Miss Parry and went after her.

"Sit down again, my dear," said Lord Ashton. "As soon as Miss Parry returns I will take you home. I am just going to send for my carriage. Will you be all right on your own for a moment?"

Tabitha nodded, feeling weak, more from the shock than from any unhappy memory it evoked. She had come to terms with the horror of Lord Sterling's death, if not with the grief it had occasioned, many years before.

Lord Ashton took her hand and gently squeezed it before leaving her alone in the box. Tabitha took several deep breaths, willing herself to be calm. After the initial shock, it was the physical sensations rather than the emotional ones that troubled her.

When Lord Ashton returned, Tabitha lifted a shamed face toward him. "I do beg your pardon. I am so very sorry to spoil your friend's play for you," she murmured. "I expect we should stay. I do not know what caused me to make such a foolish outburst over a pretend gunshot."

"I do know," he said very gently. "And if I had also known that there was such a scene in the play, I should never have subjected you to it. Kingsley told me he had added some new surprises, but he did not tell me what they were. Fortunately, my carriage is not too far away and will be here in a moment." He came to sit beside her, but did not even glace at the stage where the action of the play continued. "Miss Parry has not yet returned, I see."

"No." Tabitha made an effort to regain her composure. "I would like very much to go home, but I cannot ask you to ruin your evening."

"But it would be ruined if I could not take you home," Lord Ashton said, firmly but kindly. "And I have seen the work before. I even took the part of Sir Barnaby in an amateur production at Mr. Kingsley's home."

"But it is a very different thing, surely," Tabitha said, "to see it in a real theater, with real actors. I do not wish to deprive you of that. And you do not want to miss Mr. Kingsley's other surprises."

"If they are anything like the last one, I shall be happy to avoid it tonight. I shall be bringing my sister tomorrow night," Lord Ashton replied. "I insist on taking you home, if that is what you wish, Lady Tabitha."

"I would prefer it. If you are determined it will be no great hardship, I shall not protest any longer." It would be very comforting to have him with her, and she did not think she could enjoy the rest of the play. She still felt shaken.

"I do. I am so very sorry that you suffered such a shock," he said. "Can I hope that you are recovered somewhat? The only restorative I can offer you is another segment of orange—if the fruit has survived the excitement unscathed."

"Yes, thank you, to taking me home. I don't care for any more orange." Her heart still pounded, though. At this point it seemed easier to give in to the temptation and go home rather than try to reassemble their party and carry on for another hour or more.

Miss Parry returned to the box. "Well, Laura is settled. Her friend Pamela insists that they shall take her home afterward, and her mother quite overruled my protests. I have never seen such a rude woman. And her daughter has her manners. Very pert, if you please. I do not think that it suits the gentlemen who escorted their party, however. I gather they are expected elsewhere after the play."

"If it would not inconvenience you, ma'am, we could return once Lady Tabitha is home. Or I could come back with Lady Laura's maid," offered Lord Ashton, rising as Miss Parry came to Tabitha's side.

Tabitha was about to protest that she could not be the cause of such trouble when Miss Parry said, "I will return with you, my lord, if Tabitha feels she can spare me. Are you feeling a little better, my dear?"

Tabitha nodded.

"Excellent," said Miss Parry, and led the way out of Lord Ashton's box.

Lord Ashton gave Tabitha his arm, and they followed more slowly. Once downstairs, a chair was found for Miss Parry, and she suggested that Lord Ashton take Tabitha outside.

The air, which she had earlier thought nearly as stifling as that in the theater itself, Miss Parry now pronounced bracing and fresh. "Just the thing after a sudden start, my dear. But I shall sit here quietly and rest while we await the carriage."

Smiling, Lord Ashton led Tabitha onto the steps. "Do you still like the stars, Lady Tabitha?"

"Very much, my lord, but I am surprised that you trouble to remember a remark I made so long ago," she answered him. Her heart was pounding again, but this time with hope, not remembered dread.

"I remember a great deal," he said quietly. "We danced at Almack's, the quadrille and the cotillion. You wore that necklace and told me very prettily when I admired it that your grandfather had given it to you for luck."

"I remember not daring to eat more than a slice of that dry bread and butter for fear you would think me greedy," Tabitha said, and wished she hadn't. What a foolish thing to remind a gentleman of at a romantic moment.

"I am afraid that I didn't notice how much you ate. I was making the most of the opportunity presented by my taking you over to the refreshment table to enjoy your presence. I thought, and still think, that you are the loveliest and most engaging woman alive."

"What a wonderful compliment."

"I paid it to you once before."

"I remember," Tabitha said. "At Lady George's al fresco breakfast when I mistook her baby swans for goslings and everyone laughed, although Lady George was very kind about it. Do you remember?"

"I expect we remember very much the same things, Lady Tabitha."

They stood in silence for a moment, then Lord Ashton suddenly burst out, "Tell me, Lady Tabitha, is it true that you are going to accept a proposal from Lord Marlton?"

"No, it most certainly is not true," she said in some amazement. "Whatever made you think so?"

"I had that impression from your conversation with Lady Laura in the interval."

"My sister"—Tabitha took a deep breath as she tried to quell her mounting fury at Laura's machinations. Even if Laura had not planned to convey the impression that Tabitha was betrothed, she had no right to mention such a topic unless it was public knowledge or Tabitha introduced it herself—"inadvertently gave the wrong impression."

It was obvious Lord Ashton had misunderstood her own reply to Laura's insinuations. "It is true that he has offered for me. I have not discussed the matter with my sister, but I have refused Lord Marlton. And, if he proposes to me again, I shall repeat my refusal," Tabitha said warmly. "Nothing could persuade me to accept his offer. I do not like him. Indeed, there is . . . there is something in his manner that rather frightens me."

She realized that her dislike of Lord Marlton was leading her to a long speech that could be of no possible interest to Lord Ashton.

"I do beg your pardon, my lord," she said. "I should not run on so."

"It does not do you discredit. You do well to fear Marlton, my dear," he assured her grimly. "There is a great deal about him that should frighten you. The man's more than half-mad—though he is possibly the sanest in an even madder family. One of his cousins—but you know that sad story too well, I fear. Suffice to say, my very dearest, Marlton is no fit bridegroom for you."

"Oh, what did you call me?" Tabitha was finding it very hard to breathe. She was, she realized, poised on the brink of the future she had long desired.

"My very dearest," he repeated huskily. "You are, you know. I love you, Tabitha. I have loved you ever since we first met."

"Oh . . . my lord," she whispered, wondering—no, daring to hope—what he might say next.

"I might be wrong," he continued uncertainly, "but I had the impression that even though we had not seen each other more than a few times that you held me in some regard . . . all those years ago?"

"I did," she said softly. "Oh, I did, so much. So very much." Could you not tell? she wanted to cry. Can you not see that I still do?

"May I hope that you still have some feelings for me, my dear Lady Tabitha?" he said in a voice that was not entirely steady.

"Yes, oh, yes." Tears filled her eyes. "Always . . . there has never been anyone else for me."

"Nor for me, my dearest." He put his hand on her arm. "You will say that I have been wed . . . and you know that I had a child. I will tell you that my poor wife and I might have been very happy together, but nothing was ever able to fill that great empty space your departure left in my heart.

"It is you who have continued to haunt my dreams. It is you and you alone whom I have never stopped loving. But I fear I grow repetitious."

"I do not mind this repetition," said Tabitha. "I love you so very much that I could hear you say it again and again, all day and all night, and do the same myself. I do love you."

Tabitha had the certain impression that if they were not standing in a public place he would have taken her in a long and passionate embrace. Instead, he lifted her hand to his lips and kissed the palm.

"It is," he said, "something of an anticlimax to realize that I must take you home, my beautiful Tabitha, though I wish we need not be separated by as much as a minute. When you had to leave London all those years ago, I thought my happiness was at an end. And then when I received Miss Parry's letter saying that you did not wish to communicate with me, I feared you must hold me in disgust and—but there is no need to refine upon that now."

"No, my dearest Lionel, I may call you that, and you

will call me Tabitha, please? No more Lady Tabitha, I pray, it sounds so distant."

"Could you call me Lion? I dislike it slightly less than my given name, though I vow it sounds somewhat conceited. The dearest part I hope you will retain."

"No, my dearest, dearest Lion, there is no need. I am very sorry for the letter." Tabitha paused, wondering how to word the next part. "There was a misunderstanding on my aunt's part. I had given her the impression that I had no wish to pursue any of my London acquaintances . . . and . . . well, perhaps she overstated the case."

Tabitha wondered if her aunt even recalled what she had put in the letter. Tabitha knew now that her aunt had been desperate when she wrote it. Now that all was mended, there was no point in refining on just how strongly her aunt had turned her dear Lion away.

"Oh, my beloved, to hear my name upon your lips. I hesitate to interrupt, but I should like to point out that the carriage has arrived. At least I will have you close to me on the drive home, and can anticipate a time when you will be closer yet, my dearest. But enough, for Miss Parry is waiting."

They went together to fetch her. As they went inside Lord Ashton said, "I will come tomorrow and tell your aunt of our plans, for I do not think a carriage is the place to make such an announcement . . . or should I merely tell her of my intentions so that the news will be broken to her gradually?"

"You may tell her. She will be very pleased."

"I am glad to hear it. I had all these plans for courting you slowly, but Lady Laura unwittingly tipped my hand. I am very glad of it. Now, when I call tomorrow, perhaps we can discuss our wedding plans. All must be as swift as possible, for I am sure that you will agree we have waited far too long already!"

"I do agree," she said softly. "Oh, I do, Lion."

"You DID MAKE A quiz of yourself last night," Laura commented as she joined her sister in the dining room for breakfast. "Lord Ashton was certainly most obliging to take you home, especially when one of his best friends was having his play performed. And poor Aunt Ellen. I don't imagine she liked having to miss nearly all of the play and go back and forth from the theater all night."

Tabitha looked up from her plate of poached eggs and toast. "It was kind of Lord Ashton to bring me home. And so very kind of you to have a regard for your aunt's comfort," she commented coolly, forbearing to mention that if Laura had not insisted on staying to watch the end of the play, poor Aunt Ellen would have had two fewer journeys to make. "I hope you enjoyed the rest of the evening."

"I was very hard put to follow the action," Laura said disapprovingly. "There was considerable comment from other members of the audience. Furthermore, the actors and poor Mr. Kingsley, the playwright, heard you and were exceedingly disturbed."

"I am very sorry for that," Tabitha said regretfully. "But how did you find out about Mr. Kingsley's reactions?"

"After the play ended, Lord Ashton took us backstage and introduced us to him. Mr. Kingsley is very handsome—though not to compare with Lord Ashton. I did my best to make some excuse for you."

"That was kind of you." Tabitha smiled coolly. She had already finished her eggs and was pouring herself a second cup of coffee.

Laura gave her a disapproving look. "You do not seem in the least disturbed over the scene you created, Tabitha. Is there any tea left, or should I ring for a fresh pot?" She held out her cup.

"I am sorry, indeed, that I cried out," Tabitha said, as she filled her sister's cup. "But that shot brought back unfortunate memories."

"Papa's death took place a very long time ago," Laura said. "I was only nine. I am surprised that you still remember it after all this time."

"And I was little older than you are now, Laura. I do not imagine I shall ever forget those moments when . . . when I looked down and saw . . ." Tabitha paused and swallowed a lump in her throat.

Laura shook her head. "I expect the gunshot was startling, but you knew it was a play. . . . Really, Tabitha, don't think about it. Put it from your mind."

She grimaced slightly. "Oh, poor Lord Ashton, he must have been terribly embarrassed. I expect he did not say a word to you in the carriage."

"As a matter of fact, he did not," Tabitha said. She did not add that there had been no need for words between them. Miss Parry, apparently aware that both her niece and Lord Ashton preferred silence, had not spoken either. Tabitha had savored her joy all the way home, knowing that Lion, sitting opposite her in the darkness, was smiling as happily as she and that soon nothing would ever part them again.

"And I ended up losing my evening cloak," Laura continued. "The one I like so much. One of the footmen has gone to seek it, but I won't be surprised if he cannot find it. I expect whoever cleans the boxes has stolen it. And I still say that you embarrassed poor Lord Ashton."

"Is that what he told you?" Tabitha demanded, annoyed that Laura seemed determined to pursue the topic.

"No, my dear, it was not." Miss Parry entered the

room. "As an observer who prides herself on being easily as acute as your sister, I did not notice that he was in the least put out. He did explain to Mr. Kingsley, very quietly and privately, the reason for your outburst. Mr. Kingsley understood and was most sympathetic."

She turned to Laura. "You, my dear, are far too inclined to construct mountains from molehills. And it is your own fault your evening mantle is lost, for you should not have been running from box to box all evening."

"I went from one box to another. One of you might have remembered my cloak." Laura glared at Tabitha. "Lord Ashton did not seem at all like himself when he returned from taking Tabitha home. Even the playwright commented on his abstraction. Did you not notice it, Aunt?"

Tabitha smiled.

"I do not know what you find amusing in that, Tabitha," Laura said.

"You do seem in an odd mood this morning, Tabitha," Miss Parry commented. She paused as the butler opened the door.

"Yes?"

James coughed apologetically. "If you please, ma'am, Lord Ashton is here."

"Oh!" Laura cried. "Oh, how delightful."

"He's asked to see you and Mr. Henry. I showed him into the library."

Laura, impetuous as ever, ran from the room, brushing past a surprised James.

"I shall go, too, Aunt Ellen. I want to know why he is calling so early," she called over her shoulder.

"Oh, my dear," said Miss Parry. "Dare we hope?"

Tabitha smiled at her. "Wait and see. You won't be disappointed."

By the time they came to the library, Laura was chatting to Henry and Lord Ashton about her latest flirt. "I think he is very handsome," she said, "though not as handsome as an older man would be."

"I am glad to hear that, my dear," Henry commented.

"For my friend Cramer's father is nearly seventy, and tells me you are the prettiest little thing he ever did see. And he's a widower."

"Not that old!" exclaimed Laura. "About as old as Lord Ashton. But you gentlemen look so festive," she added. "What ever is the occasion? And am I invited?"

Tabitha had also noticed her brother's unusually neat attire. He was dressed much more carefully than was his wont. His cravat was heavily starched, forcing him to hold his chin at a rather unnatural angle. His coat, a deep blue, appeared new, and his vest, a delicate primrose yellow, was, she guessed, also new. His boots were polished to a high shine.

Lord Ashton was similarly well-turned-out. His cravat was more artistically tied than that of her brother. His coat, a dark navy blue, fitted him to perfection and his pantaloons were gray. However, as usual, it was his face that held Tabitha's eye. She was quite positive that there was no man more handsome in all of England.

"You most certainly are invited, Lady Laura. Your whole family is, in fact," Lord Ashton said.

"When is it, and what is it? A picnic? Are we going boating? Oh, do tell, do tell me, please. I shall go mad with waiting."

"And so shall we, I shouldn't wonder," said Miss Parry, "waiting for you to be quiet so that your question can be answered."

Henry winked at Laura. "Not for a while, and not what you expect."

"Oh? And what might you mean by that?" Laura asked, "Please, please tell."

"I will tell you. Ashton has come to me in lieu of William, who is the official head of the family . . . but a bit too far away to officiate in that capacity. Consequently, as his surrogate, I am doing the honors. He has offered for Tabitha's hand in marriage and I have given him my blessing which, I am certain, William will substantiate."

"Oh, my dear!" Miss Parry cried. "Oh, I am so pleased." Impulsively she embraced Tabitha and kissed her on the cheek, then held out her hand to Lord Ashton. "Congratulations, my lord."

"I would be very happy if you would call me your nephew Lion. And I would be honored if I could call you my Aunt Parry, ma'am."

"Fie, I am your Aunt Ellen, nephew."

Laura sat as if turned to stone. "I . . . I . . ." She looked wildly from Lord Ashton to Tabitha and then said, "Yes, of . . . of course, how . . . wonderful. You have my best wishes for your happiness."

"And mine, too." Henry put his arm around Laura's waist and drew her to his side. "Well, infant," he added, "you will be next, which is of course as it should be."

"Yes," Laura murmured. Then, gazing up at Lord Ashton, she added, "I do wish you happy, my lord. And you also, Tabitha. I suppose your happinesses are now one."

"I thank you, my dear," he said.

"When will the wedding take place?" Laura asked.

"I should like it to take place on the morrow, or perhaps the day after—though that is a sight too long to wait, do you not agree, my love?" He moved to Tabitha, who had also risen, and put an arm around her waist.

"I am in complete agreement," she said softly. "We should leave now."

"I trust you're joking," Miss Parry said determinedly. "It seems neither of you is thinking clearly . . . which, of course, is not surprising. And I do think a long engagement would be unwise. However, what you propose, my lord, is quite out of the question, indeed almost unseemly, even if a license could be arranged."

"Why is it out of the question, Aunt Ellen?" Tabitha asked a little regretfully.

"For a start, my dear, as you should well know, banns must be read for three consecutive Sundays, the rest of the family must be informed, and your bride-clothes must be made. You may," she added, "of course announce the betrothal. A notice can be sent to the papers for the day after tomorrow, and letters to Imogen, William, and James must be written today. The other relatives can wait until tomorrow. Now, do you wish to be married here or in the country?"

"Lord, Auntie," Henry protested. "Why all this pother? Let them go to Gretna Green."

"Henry!" Miss Parry said wrathfully. "You might prefer these hole-in-the-corner arrangements, but Tabitha must be married in St. James's Church, where, if you will remember, your parents were wed and also your brother William, or in the village church, where Imogen and poor Alice were wed."

Tabitha and Lord Ashton exchanged long-suffering looks. Then he said, "I do not want to wait as long as three minutes . . . nonetheless, it appears that Aunt Ellen has some cogent points."

Tabitha smiled lovingly at him. "I would like to argue with her, but our long acquaintance tells me that she will not heed me. Could we arrange to be married in eight weeks' time in St. James's?"

Lord Ashton loosed a long sigh. "If that is the best we can manage, then, my dear, I fear that we must wait. Could the engagement be only six weeks?" He cast an appealing look to Miss Parry. "We have waited rather a long time already."

"It could indeed." Miss Parry nodded. "But an engagement does not mean that you will have to wait alone. You are always welcome here, my lord—dear Lion."

"Believe me, my dear Aunt Ellen, I intend to take full advantage of that hospitality," Lord Ashton said and again looked lovingly at Tabitha.

"I would propose a toast," Henry said. "However, it being rather too early in the day, I will content myself with wishing you both the greatest happiness anyone can have."

Two days later, still not quite believing that she was really going to marry her beloved Lion, Tabitha sat at her dressing table as her abigail combed her hair. Laura, sitting in a chair watching the procedure, was discussing the gown she would wear as Tabitha's bridesmaid. Tabitha had agreed to only one bridesmaid.

"I think that blue silk or perhaps white . . . no, you will be wearing white, will you not?"

"I hadn't thought. I think I shall wear yellow, and you can wear blue."

"Sometimes I think you don't want to be married, Tabitha. You don't seem at all interested."

"Well, I am," Tabitha said. "But I am more interested in being Lion's wife than his bride."

"I would love to be a bride," said Laura. "I'd be queen for a day. Are you going to carry Mama's prayer book? Is it not a pity that she cannot be present?"

"Yes," Tabitha agreed with a little sigh.

"And Papa, of course, but I should not mention him," Laura said quickly. "It is far too melancholy a subject in view of your great happiness."

A comment trembled on Tabitha's lips regarding the great happiness that her sister seemed determined to quell with her recital of these unhappy memories. However, before she could voice it, there was a scratch on her door. "Yes?" she called.

Opening the door, Betsy, Laura's abigail, said, "If you please, my lady, Lord Marlton is downstairs. He wishes to see you urgently. He's in the library."

"Oh, I'm not even dressed." Tabitha sighed.

"Shall I send word you're not at home, my lady?"

"No, don't send him away, Betsy. He'll only be back later and I need to speak to him. This time, when I tell him I'm engaged to be married, he'll have to take no for an answer. Please ask him to wait."

"I'll go," said Laura.

"Thank you, dear," said Tabitha. "Don't forget to leave the door to the library open."

Tabitha was coming down the stairs a few moments later when she heard a commotion that chilled her. As she neared the bottom step, she saw Lord Marlton was dragging Laura, kicking and screaming, from the library, shouting, "If you say Ashton has her, then I'll take you. Any one of damned Sterling's litter will do."

"James!" shouted Tabitha. "Henry! Help! Marlton is

kidnapping Laura!" She ran to her sister's side and started to beat at Lord Marlton with her fists, still shouting for help.

Lord Marlton released Laura. "Well, then, take her!" he cried, violently thrusting her toward Tabitha. With a cry, Laura fell to the floor.

Tabitha heard the crack as Laura's head struck the ground. Lord Marlton turned to Tabitha, his hand raised.

Henry appeared from an upper floor, carrying a pair of dueling pistols. "Leave her alone," he demanded, and discharged a ball into the air. "The next one's for your damned heart!" he swore.

Lord Marlton fled down the stairs and wrenched open the front door, running for his life.

"I'll kill him!," shouted Henry.

"You'd better see to Laura first." Tabitha knelt next to her sister. Blood was oozing from her hair. "I fear she is hurt to death."

Henry crouched beside her, stroking Laura's white-blond hair. "I'll take her up to her room. James," he ordered the butler, who had just arrived. "Send for a physician—"

"Dr. Clarke," interjected Tabitha.

"Dr. Clarke," repeated Henry, "and for a magistrate. That man tried to kill m'sister. My baby sister." He shook his head. "Come on, Laura, I'm just going to lift you and carry you upstairs."

Laura did not stir when her brother gathered her in his arms. Tabitha saw tears standing in Henry's eyes.

=16=

"MY DEAR, I AM all agog," said Lady Daphne Fitzroy, sitting in the drawing room, looked wide-eyed at Tabitha. "Imagine attacking your poor sister. I hope she is feeling more the thing."

"She is, but she'll not stir from her chamber until the swelling has gone down. Dr. Clarke says she had a very narrow escape. Had she struck the side of her head instead of the back, she might have suffered a severe, possibly fatal, fracture of the skull."

"Oh, dear," Lady Daphne said in some distress. "How terrible for your sister. When did she regain consciousness? I wonder if she was frightened . . . when she was asleep, I mean . . . anyone would have been afraid before that . . . but she might have realized that she might not awaken ever again . . . or perhaps she just dreamed."

"Not for several hours. We were very worried." Tabitha shuddered at the memory of that terrible vigil by Laura's bedside. Aunt Ellen and she had sat on opposite sides of the bed, holding Laura's hands, while Henry, busy with the magistrate's men and sending messages to William, had crept in and out of the room to whisper with Dr. Clarke.

"That wretched man . . . he should have been clapped in prison . . . none of this dallying around waiting for evidence and a warrant . . . however, he will get his deserts and soon," Lady Daphne said sharply.

"His deserts?" Tabitha questioned. "What ever do you mean?"

"Oh, dear." Lady Daphne blushed. "I ought not to . . . to have mentioned that. Samuel would be most disapproving if he knew I had . . . he particularly asked me to keep it to myself, but well . . . you won't tell him . . . I expect you ought to know, even if he did not tell you."

"What didn't Mr. Fitzroy tell me?" Tabitha questioned.

"Not Samuel, Lord Ashton."

"Tell me about this, Daphne," Tabitha demanded, suddenly feeling alarmed.

"Well, Samuel was in White's yesterday and Lord Marlton came in . . . good heavens, he must have come there immediately after leaving here . . . so perhaps he wasn't too distraught to know what he wanted . . . did he ever say what he wanted with your little sister?"

"No, he didn't. He came into White's, and then what happened?" Tabitha prompted.

"I really ought not to worry you with this matter."

"I am already worried. What do you mean, Daphne? For goodness sake, tell me!"

"I meant to tell you when I arrived . . . I mean, I would have told you, because it is very amusing, too . . . but then I remembered what Samuel said to me. When Lord Marlton said, 'You're a black-hearted rotter, a ravisher, and a knave,' my husband said, 'Has he given you a choice or does he mean all three?' "

"I have no idea what you're talking about," said Tabitha. "Does it concern Lion?"

"Not really . . . not this part . . . Lord Marlton, such a wretch . . . I have never been able to abide him . . . Mad Marlton, he is called now and with reason—he issues challenges to people on the slightest pretext, and he nearly killed poor young Mr. Carlington. It was a real scandal, for they fought over the veriest nothing, and of course I am absolutely certain that he drove his first wife into the grave . . . such a sweet woman . . . my mother and I both knew her and we were absolutely forbidden the house when she married him.

"Yes." Lady Daphne frowned and lowered her voice. "I think he beat her . . . he has the most fiendish temper and he picks quarrels at the lift of an eyebrow. That's what Samuel said, and of course there is poor Laura—imagine knocking her down like that! Gracious, I hope she is not suffering overmuch!"

"She is not very comfortable, as I told you, but you were mentioning Lord Marlton's deserts. What precisely did you mean? If you do not tell me straight, Daphne, I shall shake you," said Tabitha.

"Well, as I understand it, he came storming into White's and knocked down Lord Ashton."

Tabitha's hand flew to her throat. "Gracious! Did he hurt Lion?"

"No, he didn't . . . but he did challenge him to a duel."

"A . . . a duel?" Tabitha paled.

"Yes, it will take place tomorrow . . . so I understand from—"

"Where?" Tabitha interrupted. "Where will they be fighting?"

"Oh, the usual place . . . Combe Wood, near Wimbledon and early, of course, around six in the morning, I should think, else one runs afoul of the law. It is fortunate they will be fighting with swords . . . I understand Marlton is a crack shot, hits the pips from playing cards . . . though I would think the hole made by the ball would be bigger than the pip, so much bigger that one couldn't tell how well one had done . . . but as the challenged, of course, Ashton had the choice of weapons. I think your brother will second him . . . he was in the club when the encounter took place."

"I see," Tabitha said, faintly.

"It is a coil, is it not? I think Lord Ashton should run him through the heart . . . of course, he would have to leave London and go to France or perhaps to Ireland . . . though no one would care for Lord Marlton . . . he has a really bad reputation . . . and you might enjoy living in France . . . but not, I think, in Ireland."

"And . . . suppose Lord Marlton were to run Lion

through the heart?" Tabitha shuddered.

"My dear, what a terrible thing to say. I beg you'll not fret . . . I doubt that he could . . . Lord Ashton, according to Samuel, is an excellent swordsman and he has had other duels forced upon him and each time he has won . . . though I suppose it would be easier to see how well one had done poking at a playing card with a sword . . . there is no reason that he will not have his usual luck in this silly quarrel."

"I . . . see," Tabitha said.

"Oh, dear, I fear I have worried you. You must not fret, Tabitha—it is Marlton who should fret. I am certain he has met more than his match . . . there is small chance that Lord Ashton will be the loser in this uneven combat because they are laying odds . . . but long shots never seem to pay. I wish they would, for then it would be so easy to be very, very wealthy."

"Combe Wood near Wimbledon, you say? It is a distance from here, I should imagine."

"True, but it is easy to find . . . at least so my husband says. I rather think they will ride out together . . . oh, I do hope Lord Ashton runs Marlton through—he is such a horrid man it would serve him right. Imagine attacking poor Laura like that . . . and you say she has a fractured skull?"

"Well." Tabitha sighed. "It is possible. She undoubtedly has a very severe concussion."

"Oh, that wretch of a man. But it is all of a piece with his other actions." Lady Daphne shook her head. "I fear I grow repetitious on the subject. I had best leave, my dear . . . and I beg you'll not worry about Lord Ashton—he'll not be the loser, I can assure you. It would be too unfair now that you are betrothed."

"I pray to God he will be safe," Tabitha said tensely as she rose.

After seeing her friend to the door, Tabitha went into the library and sank into a chair. She had been very glad to see Daphne leave.

She would pray for her Lion's safety, but she knew that the Lord helps those who help themselves.

She had to think, to plan. At least, thanks to Lady Daphne's chatter, she did know that a duel would take place, and knew the time and location as well. That duel had to be stopped! In his present mood, Lord Marlton would never fight fairly. His attack on her poor sister was proof of that!

Should the Bow Street Runners be informed? No, she quickly discarded that notion. They might arrest both men! She, herself, must find a way to stop the duel. She could go to Lord Ashton now.

No, she could not leave the house with poor Laura in such straits. Yet someone must plead with them, beg them to exercise common sense. But she thought that Lion would only offer empty words of comfort.

If only Daphne had told her about it earlier. She had so little time. Should she go to Henry? No, that idea was out of the question, for she did not know where to find him, nor did she know how to find Combe Wood. She could ask the coachman, ask him to drive her there in the morning.

No, Bartlett would never do it. He would only tell her aunt. He had been in the service of the family far too long. Then, into her mind came Timothy, the groom who served as footman with the carriages. He was London-born and knew the city through and through. She would send for him immediately.

It was still dark when Tabitha, clad in Henry's old riding clothes, her hair gathered under a cap borrowed from Timothy, met the footman by the stables.

Much to her surprise, he stared at her as if he did not know her. Then, realizing the reason for his confusion, she was happily relieved. "It is I, Timothy," she murmured. "Pray let us be going."

"Oooh, milady, I didn't know yer lookin' like that. Are you sure this is for the best?"

"Just as well you did not. And yes, Timothy, this will save a man's life. Is everything in readiness?"

"Aye, I've put Mr. Henry's saddle on Mark." He paused

and said anxiously, "Yer sure ye can ride astride?"

"I am quite sure. As a child I rode my first pony astride, Timothy, and James rides Mark when he's home, so the horse won't be bothered by it."

"That's a mercy." He gave her a dubious glance. "But it seems to me, milady, that when the quality 'as it in mind to fight wi' swords, there isn't nothin's goin' to stop 'em. T'would be better wi' fists an' less dangerous to be sure, but they doesn't seem to think so."

"I agree, and that is why I must stop this duel! Let us go at once, please."

"Milady, they'll be mad as fire. Mr. Bartlett'll 'ave my guts for garters."

"You need not be troubled by that," she said impatiently. "I shall see that no blame comes to you. Now, here's a guinea. You'll have another once we've arrived."

The ride in the darkness was one of the loneliest hours in Tabitha's life, filled with apprehension that she would arrive too late, or in the wrong place, or would meet them coming home, carrying Lion's body. When the small birds began to sing with the gray false dawn, the sound, which had always before been a promise of life and hope, sounded to her as sad as a funeral dirge.

The way to Combe Wood was longer than she had anticipated. Much to her dismay, there was soon a thin line of red across the eastern horizon and they had not yet reached their goal, having been halted more than once by lumbering drays coming into the city and herds of cattle and even ducks being driven into the Smithfield market.

By the time they came in sight of their destination, her heart was pounding heavily in her chest. The birds were now twittering loudly in the trees, the sun was fully risen, and they had yet to find Lion.

A short time later, they were alerted by the ominous sound of steel on steel. "There be a clearing yonder," Timothy said. He dismounted hastily, tethering his horse to a low-hanging branch. Glancing up at her, he added, "You stay 'ere, milady." He hurried toward the sound and for a moment was lost among the thick-growing trees. Tabitha watched impatiently, wondering if it was not best to join him.

A few moments later, he returned. "They be at it 'ot 'n 'eavy," he said excitedly. "Come, I'll 'elp ye down."

"There's no need," she said, as she slipped out of her saddle. She watched impatiently as Timothy tethered her horse to another branch.

Then with him in the lead, Tabitha hurried toward the site, a stretch of barren ground where the two men were grimly fighting, their faces reddened by the rising sun, which also glowed like blood on their clashing rapiers.

"We must stop them!" Tabitha cried.

"Can't rightfully see how, milady—not now," he said, excitedly watching the duelists. " 'Twill be over soon, it will," he added. "Marlton, 'e be overmatched."

In that same moment, Lord Marlton made a rush at Lord Ashton only to fall back. Lord Ashton's weapon flashed, quick and true, and struck down his opponent's rapier before piercing his shoulder. With a howl of rage and pain, Marlton staggered back and fell, glaring furiously at his opponent. Then, with a hasty movement, he drew a pistol from under his black waistcoat, aiming it at Lord Ashton.

"Cor, 'e can't do that, it's 'gain sportin' rules," muttered Timothy. Then, "Milady, where be ye goin'? Come back, come back 'ere right now," he yelled.

Tabitha rushed in front of Lord Ashton. There was the loud, awful sound of a gunshot, and a terrible smell of black powder.

At the same time Henry threw himself at Lord Marlton and wrenched the pistol from his grasp. He then whirled on his sister, demanding furiously, "Are you quite mad, Tabitha?"

"Yes, she is! Entirely mad," Lord Ashton said in a shaken tone of voice. Putting his arms around Tabitha, he stared angrily down into her face. "Do you imagine that I would want to live if you were to die?" he cried.

"Then imagine, sir, how I feel," she said with a flash

of anger. "Lion, oh, Lion, I was so frightened for you. Are you all right?"

"You had no need to be, my love," he assured her gently.

"The pistol?"

"The shot must have gone wild," he said confidently. Then he added, "But enough, my very dearest, neither of us is hurt. And we must put an end to this sorry matter. You stay where you are," he ordered sternly as he went to join Henry, who was glaring down at the groaning, writhing Marlton.

"You ought to be tried for attempted murder, and will be if I have any say," Henry was saying contemptuously. "In any case, you are finished here, Marlton. There is not a man who will not give you the cut direct when this sorry tale gets about."

"May you be damned and double-damned," snarled the wounded man and fainted.

The doctor came forward to examine Lord Marlton. "It is a clean wound through the shoulder and should heal easily enough, more's the pity," he said disgustedly.

"Lord Ashton." Gabriel Fitzhugh, who had been acting as Marlton's second, also came forward. "I'll see he's taken home," he said with a contemptuous glance at his fallen friend. "And that's the last thing I'll do for him."

"I thank you, Fitzhugh," Lord Ashton said, moving to Tabitha and putting an arm around her waist. "Come, my dearest love. You should not be here at all, you know, but since you are, you had better put your cap back on, tuck up your hair, and join us at the King's Head for breakfast. It is no great distance from here. And then—"

"And then, we will ride back to face Aunt Ellen's righteous wrath," Henry finished with a grimace and a laugh.

"Which might prove a sight worse than the duel," Lord Ashton commented.

"Do not doubt it," Henry assured him.

"I'll be goin' then, if yer not needin' me no more," Timothy said.

"Yes," Tabitha said quickly. "You must take Mark

home, and tell Bartlett I told you to take him out. I'll explain everything else to him later. There will be a place for me in a carriage going home, Lion?"

"There will always be a place for my brave lioness," Lord Ashton said, and kissed Tabitha thoroughly.

Epilogue

"Is HE NOT A perfect little man?" said Tabitha proudly as she handed her six-week-old son to Laura.

"Leo is a very, very sweet baby," she replied, taking the child.

"And so is your little Ellen," Tabitha declared, looking toward her aunt, who sat holding her namesake, smiling happily.

"She is perfect," said her proud papa, who was watching anxiously.

"Oh, Frederick thinks the sun rises and sets with that infant," said Laura, but her own smile was just as doting.

"And," said James, who was starting to find all the talk of babies rather dull, "they can grow up as twins, since Ellie is only three months older than Leo. And the sooner they grow up, the better, I say."

The family had gathered at Lord Ashton's country house to celebrate the first anniversary of his marriage to Tabitha and the double christening of this firstborn son and Laura's little daughter.

"Can you spare me a minute, Frederick?" Lord Ashton asked. "If you'd come into my library. . . ." The men excused themselves, but not before Sir Frederick had pressed a kiss to his daughter's forehead.

"What's all that about?" asked James.

"I expect Lion will tell us when he's ready," Tabitha answered her brother, "but I am sure that they will come here as soon as they have concluded their arrangements."

She could see that Laura was bursting with curiosity,

but instead of demanding to be told as she would have a year before, she kept silent.

Suddenly making up her mind, Tabitha said, "Imogen, would you like to take Leo awhile, or I can ring for his nurse. I want to ask Laura to come take a turn in the garden with me. It's still a warm afternoon."

"I would love a chance to pet him. I never thought I would hold a child of yours, Tabitha, and I am delighted at the prospect," Imogen replied.

It took the ladies a few moments to put on bonnets and pelisses. When they met again in the garden, Laura went at once to her sister and took her hand. "I need your forgiveness, Tabitha. I have wanted to speak to you for so long, but there was your wedding and then mine."

A month after Tabitha's well-attended wedding at St. James's Church, Laura had married Sir Frederick Perdue in the small church in his native village, with only members of the couple's families and Sir Frederick's best friend present.

"And then we both went to our husband's home, and at Christmas I never seemed to be able to get a moment alone with you. I thought maybe you were avoiding me."

"Never. I will own that you were a sore trial to me when we were in London last year, but marriage and motherhood have done wonders for your character."

"It's not merely those, Tabitha, it was Lord Marlton. I realized that I could have died when I hit my head. And what would people remember me for? I rather suspect that some would have been glad to see the end of me. You'd know that I had tried to spoil your happiness with Lord Ashton; Aunt Ellen would recall all my rudeness and thoughtlessness; and," she paused and looked away from her sister, "and I was not sure if Frederick really cared for me, or merely sported with me. I had been so absorbed in knowing that I was going to be able to force a marriage on him if I couldn't bring Lord Ashton to the point, that I had never even found out the first thing about him. I was such a horrid, wicked person."

"But why were you so eager to marry?" asked Tabitha.

It was the first time since Laura had informed them that she must be married quickly that her sister had brought the subject up.

"There was my silly vow, and I thought," Laura said simply, "that it would be fun. My husband would be so besotted that he'd let me do anything, unlike you and Aunt Ellen. Dare I hope that you don't mind that I didn't name the baby for you?"

Tabitha worked her way through the tangle of negatives of the last part of her sister's speech. "Of course not. Our aunt was very, very touched, Laura. No one had ever thought to name a child for her, after all the kindnesses that she has shown the family. It was very thoughtful of you." She sat down on a rustic bench. "Do you mind if I ask you a question, dear, about your marriage?"

"No," said Laura, sitting beside her. "It is funny how after all I was the youngest one to get married."

"Are you happy with your husband?"

"Oh, yes! I never imagined what a joy it would be to care for someone. Were you worried that because he, er, anticipated a bit, that he wasn't going to make a good husband? Well, I suppose that he was a bit rackety, but I can't imagine a kinder husband.

"I didn't plan to meet him in London, but when I first saw him I did arrange to meet him in the park. And I saw him afterward. I had an arrangement with Pamela and Cornelia. You thought I was with one of them, and both their mamas thought I was with the other.

"Lord Ashton found out. Only that we were meeting, I think, not everything. He sent word that Frederick was to come to him as soon as he could. He came that night at the opera, when we sat opposite Lord Ashton's box. I saw Frederick smiling at the dancer, and I was so cross. But do you know, Lord Ashton went and offered him money to leave me alone, and he refused. Just as he did years ago. He loved me all that time.

"And do you know, Tabitha, he is quite besotted, and would let me do anything, but I don't want to do anything shocking anymore. Isn't it funny? Of course, since we have to live so quietly, I don't suppose I could, even if I wanted to."

Tabitha reflected that the old Laura would have not let a little thing like lack of funds stand in the way of her pleasure. At first, when Laura had risen from her sickbed a quiet and biddable girl, Tabitha had suspected some new start, and waited for the fit to pass.

But a week before Tabitha's wedding, Laura's behavior was still unexceptional. Worried, Tabitha and Miss Parry had consulted Dr. Clarke, who had informed them that a change in character was not an unknown effect of a blow to the head.

"And," he added prosaically, "if being thrown to the floor by a madman isn't enough to shock a girl out of silly fits, I don't know what is."

When, a week later, poor Laura, trying not to cry, had confided to Tabitha that she could well be in an interesting condition, she apologized for telling her the night before the wedding, but she obviously still assumed Tabitha would leap to help her. That had not changed.

Still, Laura had accepted the need for a small, quiet wedding, and happily went to live on one of Lord Ashton's lesser estates in a small house and was keeping her spending inside the limits set by her brother-in-law. Of course, the fact that, as Lady Perdue and Lord Ashton's sister-in-law, she was accepted as the first lady in the small circle of country life might have given her some consolation.

"I don't imagine you ever will again," Tabitha pronounced, certain that Laura would continue to be sensible.

"And do you forgive me? I cannot tell you how sorry I am."

"Of course." The sisters embraced. Tabitha found that her eyes were full of tears. She released Laura and fumbled for her handkerchief.

"Take mine," offered Laura. "Ellie is such a messy child I always carry two or three to wipe her little face."

"Thank you." Tabitha dried her eyes. "I took you out

here to confide Lion's plan to you. I don't think you will object, but if you have any reservations . . ."

"Oh, if Frederick agrees, I shan't mind."

"Well, then, there is no point in my telling you."

"I don't mind prying into his business," Laura said, with a hint of the old mischief in her eyes.

Tabitha laughed. "I brought you out here to make sure we were not overheard. It is our little conspiracy against our husbands. Lion's brother-in-law Lord Lydford has found a position for Frederick in Canada. I know it means leaving us for several years, my dear, but it would give him a new start."

"He would like that, Tabitha. I know he would like that. Lion has been very generous, but Frederick would like to make his own way."

The sound of boots on gravel told the ladies that their husbands were about to join them. They arrived in the midst of a conversation about mulching roses.

"Guess what, my dear," Frederick cried, grasping Laura by the hand.

"I cannot imagine," she replied, wide-eyed.

"A post for me in Canada. I always knew that Lord Ashton would find something for me."

"Thank you, thank you," cried Laura enthusiastically, hugging Lord Ashton.

"Well, run along inside, children, and tell the others," he said.

Tabitha watched as Sir Frederick and Lady Perdue walked hand in hand toward the house. Sir Frederick was asking his wife how little Ellie would react to the sea voyage.

"I should have put the man in charge of an orphanage," Lord Ashton said.

"You are just as bad with Leo when you think no one is looking."

"I have been thinking, Lioness, that an entire pride might be nice."

"A little Leonie next," suggested Tabitha.

"If you like. Though I'd still love you if you'd never had

a child. Were you very frightened with Leo? Aunt Ellen seemed to think there was a family curse."

"Not really, it's just that she lost a sister and a niece in the childbed, and both were over thirty, expecting their first child. I thought . . . you might be worried, since the first Lady Ashton . . ." Tabitha did not finish the phrase.

"My dear, my first wife died of a fit three days after the child was born. The doctors assured me the two events were not connected."

"Then why . . . oh, never mind."

"You are blushing, Lioness. I would like to know why."

"Well, Henry said that you had given up opera dancers. I thought you were afraid of getting one of them with child."

Lord Ashton laughed. "I was waiting for you. The year Laura turned sixteen I hoped you would come to London. The year she was seventeen, I was in a fever of anticipation. The year she was eighteen I might have gone mad if I hadn't learned you were expected. Do you remember, I was at the house the day you came to London, trying to find out from Henry when you would arrive?"

"So you were," Tabitha said. "Do you know, I remembered nearly everything else about you, and had forgot that?"

"As long as you remember that I love you, Lioness."

"That, I'm not likely to forget. Do you think the others would miss us if we went to do something about Leonie?"

If you would like to receive details on other Walker Regency romances, please write to:

The Regency Editor
Walker and Company
720 Fifth Avenue
New York, NY 10019